SHOBHAA DÉ BOOKS

My Yummy Mummy Guide

From Getting Pregnant to Being a Successful Working Mom and Beyond

Karisma Kapoor has been one of the top actors of the Indian film industry, with award-winning performances in films like *Zubeidaa, Raja Hindustani, Dil To Pagal Hai* and *Biwi No. 1.* She lives in Mumbai with her two children.

Madhuri Banerjee is the author of national bestsellers like *Losing My Virginity and Other Dumb Ideas* and *Mistakes Like Love and Sex,* both published by Penguin Books India. She tweets with the handle @Madhuribanerjee.

Shobhaa Dé Books is a special imprint created by one of
Penguin India's best-loved and highest-selling authors.
The list will feature celebrity authors handpicked by Shobhaa,
and will focus on lifestyle, business, cinema and people.

My Yummy Mummy Guide

From Getting Pregnant to Being a Successful Working Mom and Beyond

Karisma Kapoor

with Madhuri Banerjee

Sdé
Shobhaa Dé
BOOKS

SHOBHAA DÉ BOOKS

Published by the Penguin Group

Penguin Books India Pvt. Ltd, 11 Community Centre, Panchsheel Park, New Delhi 110 017, India

Penguin Group (USA) Inc., 375 Hudson Street, New York, New York 10014, USA

Penguin Group (Canada), 90 Eglinton Avenue East, Suite 700, Toronto, Ontario, M4P 2Y3, Canada
(a division of Pearson Penguin Canada Inc.)

Penguin Books Ltd, 80 Strand, London WC2R 0RL, England

Penguin Ireland, 25 St Stephen's Green, Dublin 2, Ireland (a division of Penguin Books Ltd)

Penguin Group (Australia), 707 Collins Street, Melbourne, Victoria 3008, Australia (a division of Pearson
Australia Group Pty Ltd)

Penguin Group (NZ), 67 Apollo Drive, Rosedale, Auckland 0632, New Zealand (a division of Pearson
New Zealand Ltd)

Penguin Books (South Africa) (Pty) Ltd, Block D, Rosebank Office Park, 181 Jan Smuts Avenue, Parktown
North, Johannesburg 2193, South Africa

Penguin Books Ltd, Registered Offices: 80 Strand, London WC2R 0RL, England

First published in Shobhaa Dé Books by Penguin Books India 2013

ISBN 9780143417286

Printed at Thomson Press India Ltd, New Delhi

To my children—Samaira and Kiaan—who are my reason for writing this book, my source of happiness every day.

To my grandmother Barbara Shivdasani for showing us how to fill our kitchens with food and our lives with love. You are the epitome of elegance and my first fashion guru.

To my mom who remains a constant inspiration. Your values and morals make me who I am, and I hope to pass these on as a legacy to my children.

Contents

The Motherhood
of Travelling Pants
Of Office Bags
and Luggage Tags

The Chronicles
of Mama Mia
Of Helping Children Grow
and Growing along with Them

Acknowledgements

Thank you to the people who made this book possible:

Bebo—for being the best sister in the world, for all that you do, and your endless support and encouragement, which pushes me forward in so many ways.

Pia J. Vyas and Dr Jui Lutchman Singh—my childhood friends. Thanks for all the support over the years.

Madhuri—for penning down my thoughts and more. Thank you.

To the Penguin team—for giving me an opportunity to tell my story, a story that you believed people would want to read, and being patient until I got it right.

Thank you, reader, for picking this book up and coming into my world. I know how difficult it is to find your identity when you become a mother. Always know that I am with you and that you should believe in yourself!

Till next time.

Lots of love,
Karisma

Introduction

Born into a family that was into films, my destiny seemed set. And I loved every minute of it. I made my acting debut at the age of 16 and I did it with so much passion. From commercial films to arty ones, I tried it all. I loved the glamour, the sets and the people. But a part of me kept feeling that I was missing something. The nagging feeling didn't go away till I finally decided to get married and have children. Despite having a National Award and 4 Filmfare awards, my biggest achievement will always remain the birth of my children, Samaira and Kiaan.

I've learnt more about life from motherhood than from acting, winning awards and being in the limelight. Being a parent allows you to learn something new about yourself and another human being every day. That's life's greatest learning. The journey of any actress can be revealed on any website. But the path a mother takes is individual and personal. I wanted to share my journey with you. A journey that is filled with moments of love, laughter, doubt, fatigue, strength and perseverance—the passage of a woman from being in the public eye to becoming a nappy changer. I've been there and done it all. And I'm still learning today.

Many of my friends disagreed with me when I chose to concentrate on my children instead of films, berating me about how I was giving up a legacy. However, I continued to work even after marriage and children. I found the balance. It may not be as hectic as before, but it's far more rewarding. The path from being a svelte Bollywood actress to a pregnant woman who had put on 24 kilos during her pregnancy and coming back to the thin me was more challenging than the role in *Zubeidaa*! I wanted to reveal my secrets to everyone.

A director could always tell me what to say, what to wear and what to do on a set. As a mother, I needed to learn on my own how my body changed and what my soul needed. It was gruelling. There are some days when life is tiring and you want to give up. I can now understand each mother's feelings and relate to them better. I know how hard it is to lose weight, eat right, exercise, be happy for your kids, balance a career and still be social. I finally understand what my mother meant when she said, 'It isn't easy being a mom but it's the best thing that can happen to you.' I now appreciate her more. Motherhood made me a better woman. I wanted to share how with everyone out there.

So this book is about all those feelings. My feelings that you will not find on the Internet. My thoughts and tips on pregnancy, motherhood and life—something which no one has ever written about. This book is a legacy to my children more than my films will ever be. It is my way of holding hands with all the mothers out there, saying, 'I get you.' This book is my way of encouraging all those who are unable to find the balance and feel stressed out in their daily life, coping with motherhood. This book is my personal journey, the one that I'm most proud of. And I hope you can take something from it as well.

Great(er) Expectations

Of Conceiving and Birthing, of Preparing and Caring

Getting Pregnant

I did not believe I was pregnant when I took the first test and it showed up positive. That's why I needed to do five more to be absolutely sure.

I'd bought the home pregnancy test kits from a medical store one afternoon. As soon as I came home, I wanted to do the test. My period had been late for a week and I hadn't told a soul. I had been planning a child with my husband, yes, but it seemed quite incredible that it could happen so suddenly. When the first result was positive, I didn't believe it—sitting on the pot in the bathroom, wondering if it could be right. I used a kit from another company and checked again. Positive. But I slept on it.

The next morning, I did a few more tests. Why? Because they say that morning urine tells you the truth. As if afternoon pee has been corrupted! Same result, each time. Positive. Positive. Positive. I was pregnant! And that's when, in sheer joy, I told my husband.

He was surprised too. 'Really?' he said. 'Are you sure? Boy, that was fast!' We hadn't expected that we would get pregnant in one shot but we had. Both times! I think I know exactly when Samaira and Kiaan were conceived. I can actually put a finger on it and say, 'Yeah, that was the moment!'

Then, I told Kareena. In her regular sisterly voice, she warned me, 'Keep it quiet for some time, till you're out of the danger zone!' I love my sister for that. No matter how modern the characters she portrays on screen, deep down she believes in the traditional way of life, especially during pregnancy and motherhood. Finally, I told my mom and the rest of the family, and everyone was extremely supportive and thrilled for me. But I remember Kareena calling me the entire day and exclaiming, 'Oh my God, I'm going to be a *maasi*. Oh my God, I'm going to be an aunt!' I think the fact that she would have that particular new role in her life excited her more than any other role she's played. Later, she went on to become this strict sister, calling me every two hours to check: 'Have you eaten? Why haven't you eaten?' If she called me late at night and I took the call, she would bark at me, 'Why are you up so late?' And I'd say, 'To take your call!' And she would have nothing to say to that. It was hilarious but she was very protective about me.

The challenge was telling my director, the one person who really needed to know as soon as possible. At the time, I was working on the film *Mere Jeevan Sathi*, being directed by Suneel Darshan. I didn't know how he would react. It's not easy to put so much money into a film and then find out that your heroine is pregnant. The entire shooting schedule goes for a toss. But Suneel was extremely supportive and, in any case, most of the shooting had already been done by the time I got pregnant.

During both my pregnancies, I worked for as long as I could. I was on the sets till the sixth month when I was carrying Samaira, and the eighth month, as I was working on an ad film, when I was expecting Kiaan. I decided to be honest with my directors and producers. That was the least I could do. My first time around, I was also shooting a TV serial and had to tell them that I couldn't be on the sets for long periods. They were also very supportive. I shot for 5–6 hours at the most every day, since I was most concerned about staying safe and keeping the baby safe. They say that you should take it very easy for the first 3–4 months of a pregnancy. You should not stress over anything because you can miscarry at any time. Even when in stress, I would try to remain calm and ward it off. I took it to such an extent that I wouldn't take any stress at all, even if it meant making a small decision! After I finished the shoot, I took a sabbatical for the next 5 years so I wouldn't have to bother about anything except my baby.

I know I got pregnant easily but many of my friends, who were pregnant along with me, had been trying for a long time. Family life and children are very important to me—here are a few tips I think can help you in getting pregnant faster.

High Five: Five Tips to Help You Conceive

Tip 1: Clockwork Coitus

Start getting intimate around the twelfth or thirteenth day of your menstrual cycle, beginning the count from the day your cycle begins. If you can, have more sex—increasing the frequency will increase the chances! But don't get pressurized into doing so and never ever pressurize your husband by saying 'let's try' and stressing him out on those very days. He just won't be able to perform if you're going to be a nag about it! If you can go on a quick vacation around those days, do so—you will both be more relaxed while trying.

Tip 2: Am I Okay? Are You Okay?

Both you and your husband should undergo physical and fertility tests so you know that everything is okay with you. At times, a hormonal imbalance needs correction before you can try to conceive. You can also get a sonography done by an infertility specialist to find out the ideal date to conceive.

Tip 3: Eat to Expect

While trying to get pregnant, don't smoke, don't drink alcohol and, in any case, don't do any drugs since all these harm the fertility process. Include fresh fruit in your diet and start eating healthy. Limit your sugar and caffeine intake. Fizzy colas and too much coffee do not help either. Keep your weight in check. If you are healthy, your body responds well.

Tip 4: Back to the Basics

Keep lying on your back after intercourse for the best effect. While you should have fun during the process, lie back and relax for some time once you're through. You can even try yoga asanas that allow you to lift your legs in the air.

Tip 5: Other Options

If, after a few months of trying in vain, you feel extremely frustrated and tired and it's taking a toll on your marriage, consult your doctor for alternative methods of conception. Both intrauterine insemination (IUI) and in vitro fertilization (IVF) can increase your chances by 20–50 per cent over the regular method. There's nothing wrong with any of these methods and you can continue having intercourse while the process continues, though you may need to check with your doctor if it's all right to have sex after conceiving.

The first time I went for a sonography, there was this one question I desperately wanted to ask. So once the doctor put the cold jelly on my belly and tried to find the baby's heartbeat, I blurted out, 'Am I having twins?' The doctor thought about it because he didn't know whether I wanted twins or not. When he finally said no, I was so disappointed. I've always wanted twins. I know it's double the work but it's also double the fun. The second time around, while I was still thinking of getting pregnant, I went to my doc and asked, 'How can I conceive twins?' He looked at me and replied drily, 'By praying!' I didn't go for any alternative methods as I didn't want to play with fate.

I wanted to have my first child before I turned 30. Doctors recommend that you should have your children before the age of 30 because your fertility is at its highest during that period. Personally, I feel that you have more energy to stay awake, run around with your child, play with him, and simply enjoy being a mother. Your body also responds well and gets back into shape easily when you're in your 20s or early 30s.

The second time I got pregnant I did the same five tests and confirmed with my doctor. This time, I didn't tell anyone. I waited for a family dinner that happened a week after I was sure and then I broke the news to everyone. Believe me, my mother was the most thrilled. Every now and then, she asks me if I'm going to have a third child but I'm more than happy with just two!

With my second pregnancy, I didn't need to proclaim to the whole world that I was expecting. Generally, I like to keep things quiet because I really believe in *nazar* (the evil eye). Yup, I am superstitious and I do believe in all those old wives' tales, every last one of them, down to not eating papaya when you're pregnant as it's very 'heaty', thinking happy thoughts only, and looking at very cute baby pictures. They may sound silly but, deep down, I believe them and I acted on each one of them.

We women have so many queries, thoughts and anxieties when we get pregnant or are trying to get pregnant. I've tried to address the most common ones below, based on my experience.

When do I know if I'm pregnant?

Believe it or not, 2 weeks are already over by the time you discover that you're pregnant. That's because your pregnancy starts on your last menstrual period (LMP) and not when you discover that you are late. Take a home pregnancy test if you miss your period by a few days. If it is positive, well, by then you would probably be in your third week! If it's negative, wait for a week before you take another test. Alternatively, you can go in for a blood test, which would be most accurate 10 days after you miss your period. Every woman has a different experience—my mom didn't know that she was carrying Kareena till she was 3 months into her pregnancy, while I knew immediately both times that I was pregnant.

We're trying but I'm just not getting pregnant. What's wrong?

You cannot conceive if your man gets unduly stressed. He gets all anxious and thinks, 'Oh God! Now I *have* to make this happen,' and it never happens. The best thing to do is rather old-fashioned—just leave it to God, keep your mind open and enjoy yourself. And then, when it has to happen, it will happen.

How do I know the due date of my baby?

Once you confirm that you're expecting, you will want to know your due date. The average length of a pregnancy is 40 weeks, or 280 days, from the first day of the last normal menses. To calculate the due date, simply add 9 months and 7 days to the date, and bingo, you've got it.

Here's how it works: say the first day of your last normal menstrual period was 1 January. Add 7 days to that number, and you get the number 8. Add 9 months, and you get October. Your expected due date is 8 October. (Some physicians use the term 'expected date of confinement', or EDC for short, to describe the due date.) Rarely is a child born naturally on his or her EDC. Most babies are born in a 10-day window before or after. This is normal. We'll come to it later.

I'm pregnant. Yay! What now?

Meet your doctor to confirm the news, and establish your due date medically. Share your happiness with your partner and family. Take deep breaths, revel in your achievement and new status, and enjoy the moment. In the next chapter, I'll explain the week-by-week development of the baby inside you.

It was an accident and I don't want it!

You might feel that you have an impossibly heavy workload and just can't manage the hassle of a child. Take time to consider it. It's easy to get an abortion and continue with your life but it takes a toll on your reproductive system and plays havoc with your mental health. Consult your doctor and understand your options. You don't need to make a hasty decision. Have a baby for yourself and not because your partner wants you to or doesn't want you to. Sometimes, an accident is a blessing in disguise. It gives you time to think.

I don't want to lose my figure!

Well, your body will change and you will have a beautiful baby bump. But you will also be able to lose it once the baby is out. I have lost 24 kg after each pregnancy and gone on to do a film after my second child! I am proud to bear the scar of a caesarean section (C-section) on my body. It reminds me of how strong I was and what a beautiful thing I did by bringing a child into this world. Your figure will go back to normal within a year. It's nothing but a blink of the eye if you consider that you are going to live for at least 70 years!

What if I'm not a good mother?

It's natural to worry that you will not be able to look after your child. It's more natural not to feel maternal at all, perhaps not even want the child. But these are biological symptoms emerging from an emotional response. You have been able to look after yourself so well all these years. You are able to look after and cherish the people around you. So why should you feel that you won't be able to look after the baby who you will love the most? Take a deep breath and relax. Pregnancy is a wonderful thing. Even if you adopt a child, motherhood is the best gift you can give yourself.

My husband is panicking. How can I help him?

There are many books in the market that advise a man to take it easy and look forward to a woman's pregnancy and the birth of a child. You can help him by telling him to stay calm and letting him know that your body knows what it's doing. He should be supportive and take good care of you. Actually, you should milk it a little and boss him around while you can! Tell him you will love him even after the baby comes, that he will always be your first love. He needs some reassurance too. Meet the doctor together. Find time for each other and read about the growth of your baby together. It will help you two connect and it will calm him down. Spend quality time together because when the baby comes, you will get very busy.

Pregnancy or adoption? Will I bond with someone else's child?

This is a very personal decision. I think every child deserves love and care and motherhood doesn't come from just giving birth. Love is unconditional when it comes to mothers and their children, no matter where they came from. If you and your partner adopt a child and give him or her all the love in the world, it is the noblest thing you can ever do. But if one of you feels that you will not be able to love the child as your own, you should consider donating to a charity that looks after children rather than bring one home and be unfair to him or her. Ultimately, this is between your partner and you. But, of course, you will have a bond with your child if you choose to adopt.

Affirmation

I will listen to my doctor.

I will trust my body.

I will be happy about being pregnant.

I will not stress or fret.

This is a new phase in my life and I welcome it!

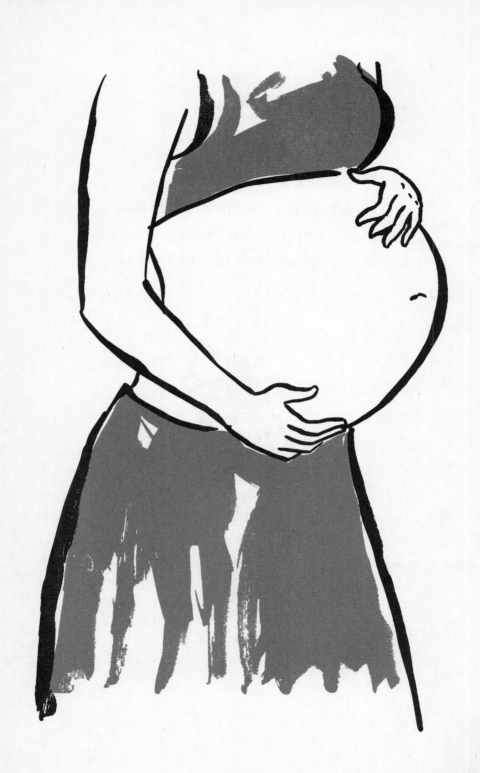

The Whole
Nine Months

No one understands the difference between weeks and months better than an expecting mother. When people asked me which month of pregnancy I was in, I would categorically answer in weeks. That is because your body changes every week! You should be proud that you hold a baby inside you, that it grows week by week, that you take such good care of it week after week. Miscarriages can occur between weeks 8 and 12 and again between weeks 20 and 25—you must be extremely careful during these weeks. In fact, many women choose not to disclose that they are pregnant till they have crossed these weeks. There's nothing wrong in keeping your pregnancy to yourself and your immediate family. It is yours after all and you can be as secretive about it as you like. It's your time to shine! And people will respect your right to privacy.

Here are some of the things that you can expect and prepare for in each trimester of your pregnancy:

First Trimester: Weeks 1 through 12

- **Doctor Hunt:** If you already have a gynaecologist who you are comfortable with, who gives you adequate time and assurance, continue to consult him or her. But if you have been dissatisfied in the past, now is the time to find a new doctor who will be patient with you and answer all your queries. You must also check out where the doctor practises. Check if the nursing home or hospital has adequate facilities and will help take care of your child and you if you go into preterm labour or need extra assistance. Speak to your friends who have had good and bad experiences before you take a call. Don't go to the most popular doctor in town—go to someone you are comfortable with. If at any time during your pregnancy you think that you need to change your doctor, feel free to go to someone else. This is your pregnancy and your child. You aren't obliged to go to your mum's gynaecologist!

- **Morning Sickness:** This is actually a misnomer. You may experience nausea at any time of the day. This can continue even into your second trimester. Don't get agitated. Your child will get enough nutrition if you take all your prenatal vitamins and eat every two hours regularly. Try and take in enough protein and stay away from strong smells that might trigger the nausea. Have light herbal teas and plenty of water. Keep light crackers in your workplace and around you.

- **Body Changes:** Your belly is going to grow but it varies from woman to woman. Don't panic if you're putting on too much weight. It could be from bloating and gas. Also, don't panic if you're not showing yet. There will be plenty of time for that. If your doctor says you're doing well, relax and keep doing what is recommended. You may tend to forget things, want to urinate more, and get acidity too often. All these symptoms are normal during pregnancy, so take them in your stride.

- **Testing Times:** Your doctor will ask you to undergo a bunch of tests to check if everything is okay with you. She will ask for your family medical history. Be sure to tell her every detail of any earlier pregnancy, illness in the family, health problems, and medicines you take. Ask questions about how much you should exercise and what vitamins you should start with. Also ask for a morning-sickness medicine even if you don't have any symptoms right now, so that you don't need to call her in the middle of a busy day if you feel sick suddenly. If you are on any other medication, do mention it to your doctor so she can prescribe the correct dosage for your pregnancy.

- **Moody Blues:** You will have those dreaded mood swings as well as constipation, gas, heartburn, weight gain and cravings for strange foods. These are all normal. Change your diet if you can figure out which foods cause them. Eat lighter foods, and eat every two hours. (More on this in the chapter 'I'm Not Fat, I'm Pregnant: The Pregnancy Diet'.) Speak to your support group (husband, mother, sister, cousin, friend) about what you're going through. Try to distract your mind from the things that make you feel low or negative.

• **Work Wise:** By this time, you will be wondering whether or not to tell your boss that you're pregnant. I am all in favour of letting your boss know once 12 weeks are up. This way you can figure out with him or her the scope of work you can take up without too much stress on you or the organization.

• **Diet Rules:** Limit your caffeine intake. It hinders iron absorption. I totally gave up coffee when I was expecting, both times. I missed it the most but I knew it was good for my children. They're very happy and healthy kids and it was a small price to pay for their well-being. Obviously you should stop smoking, and drinking alcohol, immediately, for they result in birth defects.

• **Pet Problem:** It is recommended that pregnant women should not have animals in the house. But if you've had a pet for many years, it will be difficult to let it go. Check with your doctor on the precautions you need to take for dog hair or kitty litter. These shouldn't cause any harm to the baby or you. After all, your child will be your legacy and you want to do the best for her.

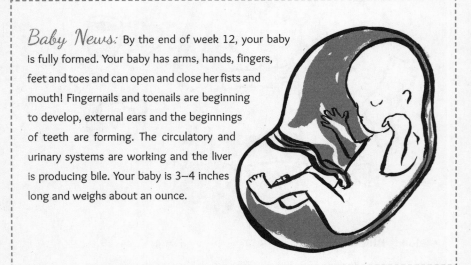

Baby News: By the end of week 12, your baby is fully formed. Your baby has arms, hands, fingers, feet and toes and can open and close her fists and mouth! Fingernails and toenails are beginning to develop, external ears and the beginnings of teeth are forming. The circulatory and urinary systems are working and the liver is producing bile. Your baby is 3–4 inches long and weighs about an ounce.

Second Trimester: Weeks 13 through 27

- **Baby Bump:** By now your morning sickness will have probably subsided and you will feel like eating more. Your belly will start to show—you should flaunt it proudly! Sometime now, you will probably feel the first kick—what fun! Soon enough you're going to have a child playing football inside your tummy though. It's all good for the development of the child and you should be happy that he is happy. Don't get anxious if he takes time to kick or doesn't kick all the time. Sometimes, babies sleep inside too. And they have no sense of time or day or night. Some babies are awake through the night. So be patient. The larger he gets, the more he will kick.

- **Shopping Time:** You can now go out and buy some maternity wear and accessories. Buy a few nice dresses that you can show off your baby bump in, as also some good bras that will support you through your pregnancy. You may need to buy some flat shoes if you've been wearing high heels all the time. Flats help you balance; you don't want to tip over with that growing belly! Remember the mantra—it's good for your back if you wear flats.

- **Travel Tips:** If your doctor says that your pregnancy is going well, this is the best time to travel with your husband.

Go on, spend some quality time together before your baby comes. But please don't go on any bumpy roads across the countryside and definitely don't go on a motorbike! Take an easy flight to a nice destination to relax and get intimate (with your doc's permission, of course).

• **The Good Life:** Spend some time by yourself, watching your favourite films, reading good books and listening to music that you enjoy. I remember I saw several romantic movies and many sitcoms while I was pregnant. It helped me pass my time so beautifully that I didn't even realize where the weeks and months went. I would listen to soothing music often. In fact, I would put on chants every morning. And it worked!

• **Womb Worries:** Consult your doctor if you get a headache, fever or palpitations. Don't take over-the-counter medicines as you never know what may harm your child. If you feel like you are getting contractions, have excessive leaks that you think are urine, or if you start to bleed, immediately rush to the hospital emergency for a check-up. Otherwise, don't psych yourself into worrying about the child. If he is kicking away, it means that you're taking enough rest and good food with your prenatal vitamins and that there's no need to worry.

• **Varicose Veins, Stretch Marks:** If you sit for several hours at a stretch, you will develop varicose veins—bluish-purplish veins bulging on the skin surface—in your legs. Walk around for 5 minutes every hour and keep your weight within the recommended limit, taking into account the baby's growth. (More on this in the chapter 'I'm Not Fat, I'm Pregnant: The Pregnancy Diet'.) Elevate your feet whenever possible and try to sleep on your left side. To prevent stretch marks from the day you know you're pregnant, rub a mixture of aloe vera and vitamin E oil into your skin twice a day when your belly starts swelling. Also, keep your tummy moisturized with cocoa butter so that the skin doesn't get dry. (More on this in the chapter 'Body Beautiful: Fitness during and after Pregnancy'.)

• **Support Group:** This is the time you may need to tell your co-workers to help you a little bit in picking things up or doing some extra work on your behalf. Ask your partner to help around the house and manage your older baby (if you have one) or just be around you to make you feel better. Tell your family what you need and where to get it from. Ask your friends to come visit you so you can catch up. The more people you have around you to seek help from and to connect with, the more relaxed you will feel. Don't stress over anything. Get enough sleep.

- **Emotions Unlimited:** There are many women who hate being pregnant or just don't feel 'maternal enough'. They may not want to lose their figures. Or they may feel that they don't have what it takes to be a mother and start to panic. Some may feel nothing at all. I have heard women say things like 'It's not affecting me at all. I know there is a baby inside me but I don't feel anything.' I'd say, DO NOT WORRY. It doesn't matter right now. Just concentrate on yourself and the rest will follow. Do not try to diet at this point and don't over-exercise to keep your flat abs. Your stomach is going to expand but it will also get back into shape later. You will become maternal and you will have enough help. If you don't feel like talking about your pregnancy, steer the conversation towards what excites you. If you don't feel like talking at all, be blunt and say so!

- **Sleepless Nights:** With your growing belly, heartburn and stress, you may experience sleepless nights, perhaps many. Try sleeping on your left side or in any position that is comfortable. Get more pillows to prop up your feet, your stomach and your head. Keep some nice-smelling incense or perfume sticks in your room; try lavender and camomile to calm you. Do not watch films or get excited right before your bedtime— watch TV only if it relaxes you. Try to get at least 8 hours of sleep every night. If you can, catch a nap during the day as well. The more you rest, the better for you.

- **The Dark Line:** Technically, it is called *linea nigra*, which means 'black line' in Latin. This is a dark, thin and pretty straight vertical streak that may appear sometime in the second trimester, running from just above the pubic bone via your navel and going as high as your lowest rib. For most women, it stops near the belly button. The linea nigra is usually 1 cm wide and fades away a few months after the pregnancy. To prevent it from getting darker, stay away from the sun, wear ample sunscreen and increase your intake of folic acid after consulting the doc.

- **Cervix Challenge:** If you have a history of second-trimester miscarriage because your cervix is weak (or incompetent, as it is called), you will be offered a cervical cerclage (a closing stitch surgically placed around the cervix). Ideally, this should be done in week 14, but it can also be done around weeks 20–23. Taken as just a precaution to see you through your pregnancy, it is a fairly simple and safe procedure done under anaesthesia.

- **Lamaze Classes:** Some birthing educators offer Lamaze classes for you and your partner to start learning the breathing techniques that can help you deliver your baby naturally. These are really good to help you stay calm and focused.

• **Losing Hair:** The hormonal changes, inevitable during pregnancy, are going to make you lose hair. Don't worry—you are not going to go bald! An average person loses 100 strands of hair a day anyway. If you lose a few more, it's no cause for panic. This will stop once the baby is born. There is also a chance that your hair starts getting thicker and more lustrous but it will start to fall out a bit after the delivery. There is no need to get alarmed in either scenario. It is due to hormonal changes and it will start to stabilize as soon as the baby is out.

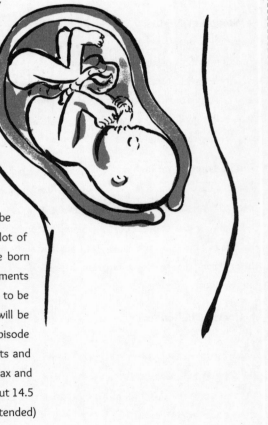

Baby News:

By week 27, your baby is sleeping and waking at regular intervals, opening and closing her eyes, and perhaps even sucking her fingers. With more brain tissue developing, your baby's brain is very active now. While her lungs are still immature, they would be capable of functioning—with a lot of medical help—if she were to be born now. Any tiny, rhythmic movements that you may feel now are likely to be a case of baby hiccups, which will be common from now on. Each episode usually lasts only a few moments and it doesn't bother her, so just relax and enjoy the tickle. Your baby is about 14.5 inches long now (with legs extended) and weighs almost 2 pounds.

Third Trimester: Weeks 28 through 42

- **Body Changes:** You will now find it difficult to run around, pick things off the floor, or even lower yourself into a chair. Take your time, take your space. There is no hurry. Don't stretch yourself too much at work or at home to finish a number of chores. Find your centre of gravity, wear flat shoes and comfortable clothes, and do things gradually, at your own pace. You will also have more heartburn and will need to make frequent trips to the loo. Eat regular meals and walk a little every day. It will all be just fine.

- **Driving Dilemma:** You may now find it tough to drive, what with the big belly in the way! So try to have someone drive you around. You definitely don't want any jerky movements in case something hits your stomach and causes pain.

- **Head Fixing:** Slowly, you'll start to wonder if your baby is a breech (legs down) or has its head down. Well, the thing is that your baby is moving all the time and will take his own time to move down for the delivery. Don't get alarmed if things are not going as per your plan. Everything takes time and your doctor will know what to do.

- **Birthing Process:** Natural or caesarean? Many women, perhaps even your doctor, will recommend that you have a natural delivery. It is the safest way and you heal and recover faster if it is natural. You can opt for an epidural (local anaesthesia to eliminate sensation, and thus pain, in the pelvic area and lower limbs) as it can pretty much halve your labour pains. But don't be afraid of the labour pains. If you have been going for your Lamaze classes and feel a lot of strength and inner peace, you must go in for a natural delivery. Opt for a caesarean only if something is wrong with the child or the doctor feels that you are at risk. I had both my children by caesarean section because, in both cases, the umbilical cord was tied around the baby's neck and it was important to loosen and release it before taking the baby out.

- **Pack Your Bags:** Be ready with your bags packed for the delivery room. You will not have time when you go into labour. Pack in some loose clothes and undergarments, a mild deodorant, toiletries, a comfy nightgown or pyjamas, slippers to pad about in in the hospital room, nursing bras, nursing pads, sanitary napkins, baby clothes (especially caps and mittens), diapers, extra cloths for burping and cleaning, a hand sanitizer for anyone who wants to hold the baby, a box of tissues, some hand towels, a top-up milk box with bottles, a sterilized nipple for newborns and a bar of nice-smelling soap.

- **False Contractions:** Braxton Hicks contractions are also called false contractions because they make you feel like you're experiencing contractions even though you're not really in labour yet. True labour contractions will get longer in duration, closer in frequency, and stronger in intensity while false contractions might get closer together, though not consistently, or may get stronger but may also go away if you move around. And then there are some moms who only experience Braxton Hicks contractions when moving around, not when they sit down!

- **Name Game:** The third trimester allows you to spend some time preparing for your baby. We will discuss this in later chapters but it's always fun to pick a boy's name and a girl's name at this time so you can start calling your baby by name when he or she is born. Otherwise, those pet names which you improvise tend to stick and you, or the child, might not appreciate them later!

- **Body Treatments:** This is a good time to get a few massages that don't touch your stomach. Sit up and get a back massage. Get your arms and feet massaged every day. Stimulating certain nerves around the ankle can expedite contractions so stay away from invigorating pedicures but do get your toenails trimmed and skin buffed so you can feel pretty. Get a nice manicure too. And oh, get yourself waxed and cleaned before you go into labour as there will be many pictures of you and your baby!

- **Leaks Galore:** Time for leaky breasts and bladders! Your body is preparing for the birth. Your mammary glands have been activated and are getting your breasts ready to feed the baby. With your girth expanding, there's pressure on your bladder and you may feel some incontinence. Practise your Kegel exercises (to strengthen the pelvic floor) and don't delay visits to the ladies' room. All will be back to normal soon.

- **Examination Redux:** You will need to visit your doctor more frequently after week 32 to see how well the baby has formed and when you will be ready to deliver. The due date may shift now so don't be alarmed if it's earlier than you thought it would be. Wrap up all your chores and take out some time to relax before the birth of your baby. Nothing should be more important than your safety and comfort at this time.

- **Work Wise:** This is the time to hand over charge to someone else since you won't be thinking straight for some time after the baby comes. Train your juniors/partners/colleagues to take over your workload till you return from your maternity leave. Most mothers work till the day they deliver but I would recommend that you stay at home from week 34 or 35 to just relax and prepare. If you like keeping busy and are fit, then keep working till a week before the due date.

• **Emergency Numbers:** Keep all emergency numbers handy. Save the numbers of your doctor, nursing home and family on speed dial, just in case you are stuck somewhere and you go into labour. This is highly unlikely but since I'm in the movies, I cannot rule out the possibility!

Baby News: By week 31, your baby will get signals from all five senses. He will perceive light and dark, taste what you eat and hear the sound of your voice. During week 34, a baby boy's testicles start their downward journey from abdomen to scrotum. By week 36, you've got about a six-pounder in there, with fat continuing to accumulate. With every week that passes, the baby has better chances of survival but there is nothing that says a baby can't be born preterm and not survive. I have a friend whose baby was born in week 28 and is a very healthy boy today.

Signs You Must Not Ignore!

- Baby not kicking enough (once he has begun to move regularly)
- Severe or persistent pain in the abdomen
- Spotting or bleeding
- Increased vaginal discharge or change in type of discharge (turns watery, mucousy or bloody, even if it's only pink or blood tinged)
- Pelvic pressure (a feeling that your baby is pushing down), menstrual-like cramping or abdominal pain, or more than four contractions in an hour (even if they don't hurt) before week 37
- Painful or burning sensation while peeing with little or no urine
- Severe or persistent vomiting, or any vomiting with pain or fever
- Chills or fever above 100°F
- Any visual disturbances (double vision, blurring, dimming, flashing lights, 'floaters')
- Persistent migraines or any headache with blurred vision, slurred speech or numbness
- Leg/calf cramps that don't ease up when you flex your ankles or walk around
- Significantly increased swelling in one leg compared to the other
- Any trauma to the abdomen
- Fainting, rapid heartbeat or palpitations
- Difficulty in breathing, shortness of breath, coughing up blood or chest pains
- Severe constipation with abdominal pain or severe diarrhoea for over 24 hours
- Itchiness all over the body
- Flu exposure or symptoms (fever, sore throat, cough, runny/stuffy nose, fatigue, body ache, chills, occasional vomiting or diarrhoea)
- Sudden dizziness or confusion
- Reduced foetal movement
- Exposure to a communicable disease like rubella or chickenpox
- Severe depression

Affirmation

Pregnancy is a beautiful phase to be in.

I am experiencing a human being grow inside me.

I must look after myself because I have the power

to choose between what's good and what's not.

Of Baby Showers, Nurseries and Nannies

The Baby Shower: It's Raining Love and Blessings!

In India, the baby shower has a bunch of traditional versions, like *godbharai* across north India, *shaad* in Bengal, *seemantham* in Kerala, and *valaikaapu* in Tamil Nadu. In Hindi, godbharai literally means 'to fill the lap', with love, with abundance, with blessings! It is celebrated after the seventh month of pregnancy. It's literally like a wedding sangeet where the elder women of the family give jewellery and clothes to the young mother-to-be while her friends entertain her with songs and stories of their own pregnancies and children.

Frankly, I'm a very private person and I really believe in nazar so I didn't have a lavish baby shower. For Samaira, I had only one godbharai in Delhi, only to please family members, but nothing in Mumbai, and the second time for Kiaan, I didn't have any of it at all. All my friends and family would ask, 'Can we arrange a baby shower for you?' But I'm very uncomfortable accepting so many presents. I know that's an odd thought but that's just me as a woman. I just feel very uncomfortable being the centre of attention and accepting so many gifts from everyone!

But these days, a baby shower is essential for pregnant women. They feel pampered and blessed, as many of their friends and family members come and bond at this time. I have attended all my friends' baby showers and loved them all. Generally, it is the mom-to-be's closest friend or sister or a family member who organizes the shower for her. If I had to have a baby shower, I'd do it this way:

Shower Settings

- **Something Simple:** I'd love to have a simple baby shower at home with just my closest friends and family. But if it's too much stress to organize everything at home, hire a banquet hall and call everyone you want. Do order a special baby-shower cake though. If you're celebrating at home, put up some balloons and streamers to make it festive. Find a friend who can take photographs or hire a photographer to capture those special moments.

- **Gift Registry:** There might be a few stores that you've visited and where you've liked a few things for yourself and the baby. You can ask the store to hold on to those things for you and start a gift registry. In the shower invite, let people know where to pick up gifts from. You might feel it's quite shameless to ask for things, right? Believe me, your friends really want to gift you something useful but don't know what, so it's better to let them know. You don't want to be left with duplicates of things that you don't even want!

- **Shower Games:** Since it is a baby shower, you must have little games for everyone to enjoy. Games can include bets on whether it is a boy or a girl, best or funniest names that everyone can come up with, and so on. Finish with a song-and-dance ritual for everyone to perform so that the momma-to-be is left happy and radiant at the end of it all.

- **Dress-Up Diva:** You may want to wear something new on your shower as photographs of this day will be kept to show your child later who all came to bless him. Be comfortable in your new attire and make sure you dress according to the season.

Don't wear a flimsy dress if you're having a shower in the winter in Delhi! A flower maxi dress looks cute and lets you show off your baby bump too. If you're attending a baby shower, wear something pretty yet simple, like a salwar-kameez or a kurti with jeans. You don't want to upset the expectant mom by showing off your new, figure-hugging designer ensemble!

• **Giving Gifts:** I often take gift baskets that I've put together myself. I include little bibs, bottles, pacifiers, dresses, blankets, sterilizers, bedding, toiletries, and small chocolates for the mom-to-be. These are all useful things, I feel. Don't gift anything that will be stressful for her to look after like a new pup or a goldfish! At times, flowers can cause pollen allergy so it's best to avoid those and give chocolates or brownies instead. Photo frames, baby books, a recorder to tape the baby's sounds perhaps, a baby monitor, bouncy chair, baby sling, pram or even a simple musical toy to hang over the baby's cot and soothe him to sleep are great ideas for gifts. Whatever you gift, make sure your name is on it and let the mother-to-be know that you'd be willing to exchange it if she has a duplicate. You don't want her running around to find a replacement if she's been gifted two prams for one child!

• **Finger Foods:** No one expects a six-course dinner at a baby shower. Serve simple and tasty finger treats. Sandwiches, pastries, tarts, quiches, fish fingers, chicken tikkas, dhoklas, idlis and cupcakes are just right for this occasion. Baby showers are like a high tea or the first of a child's birthday parties, usually held between 5 p.m. and 8 p.m., right before dinner for most people. So you can serve some mocktails, tea, coffee and fruit juices along with the snacks. Some people like to have an elaborate lunch and some like to keep it simple and light—go with what is convenient for you.

Many families, like mine, don't like to shop for babies in advance. They consider it inauspicious. So what you can do—and that's what I did—is to choose everything, pay for it but not pick it up just yet. When you come back home from the hospital, you can ask a family member to pick it all up or you can ask the store to bring it over to your home that day. But don't leave everything for after! You should pick up certain clothes and, of course, that cloth for burping the baby and the diapers and some clothes because you will need those at the hospital as well. Also, when you bring the baby home, you should have something ready to be used! I picked up the basics for the baby. The rest came later.

Baby Basics: Fifteen Things to Pick Up before Your Delivery

1. Nappies
2. Sterilizers
3. Burping cloth (to put over your shoulder)
4. Baby clothes (ideally front-buttoning)
5. Diaper-rash cream
6. Hand sanitizer
7. Baby blanket
8. Roll of cotton or cotton balls
9. Baby soap and shampoo
10. Baby hairbrush
11. Mittens
12. Baby clothes' detergent
13. Sterilizing liquid
14. Feeding bottle
15. Flask for boiled water

Oh, and don't worry if you're having a boy or a girl. It hardly matters that you've dressed your son in pink outfits. He doesn't care right now as long as he's covered. And he's going to look cute, no matter what. Buy some clothes and accessories in neutral pastel colours like yellow, peach and lime if you're concerned about what people will think.

If you have an older child, don't forget to pick a gift for her, which you can give when you get back home from the hospital. Later, you will get so immersed in looking after your newborn that your older child might feel neglected. Giving her something to keep her occupied is a wise idea.

Put on Hold: Ten Things You Should Have but Can Buy Later

1. Breast pump
2. Swaddling cloth
3. Feeding pillow
4. Baby sling
5. Baby wipes
6. Baby bathtub
7. Towels and small washcloths
8. Stroller
9. Bouncy seat
10. Car seat

It's easy to get carried away and buy everything you want for the baby. Things in small packages look adorable—but they all add up! It creates junk in your house and you're soon left with many unused things that are mighty expensive. So wait till the baby comes and then figure out for yourself what the things you definitely need are. I would advise you to not get carried away by buying things to show off to others. Many new parents buy expensive prams and designer clothes and even do up the nursery so that the people who come to visit are impressed. This is the beginning of your life as a mother and it doesn't matter if you don't have everything that someone else had when they had a child. Be sensible and save up for your child. He'll need many things as he grows.

The Nursery: A Room to Call My Own

Luckily, I had a spare room, which I could do up for the baby. So when I was pregnant with my first child, Samaira, I converted it into a nursery, did it up in a pastel yellow palette, and put in many things that I thought she'd like. It's great to have a separate room for the child, because then you have your own space, the baby has its own space, and sleeping becomes much easier and undisturbed. When there is an older child, she will have separate timings and it is important to keep them separate so that she is not disturbed. Also, the baby gets more comfortable within his space and it can become his room later on. I love doing up interiors. While I was pregnant with Kiaan, I did up my Mumbai home, and kept myself very active throughout my pregnancy.

Nursery Needs: Ten Tips for the Lil One's Den

1. **Dream Theme:** Choose a soft pastel palette that is neutral, like yellow or pistachio green or eggshell white. On one wall, you can put up wallpaper that is pleasing to the eye—with cartoons or flowers or small motifs. You can even get wall stickers and make your own mural, with a fable theme or a beach theme (with seashells). Whether you put up rainbows or butterflies, cartoon characters or solid stripes, teddy bears or hearts, or just a combination of two colours, make it harmonious with all the elements of the room. Do stay away from the room while it's being painted though—you don't want to inhale toxic fumes, especially while you're pregnant!

2. Rocking Chair: You will probably cuddle the baby to sleep in the nursery and you'll need to keep your feet up. Since babies like to be rocked, it's nice to have a rocking chair or feeding chair that is comfortable for you and the baby. Get one with a footstool.

3. Closet/Drawers: Baby things take up a lot of space. You must keep separate spaces for them.

4. Cosy Crib: You may not want to keep the baby in a crib in the beginning but don't get into the habit of keeping him next to you while you sleep. Children get used to a particular space. You can put him down in his crib with some soft, soothing music while he sleeps. Then the bed is free for you to move around in. Or you can get a bassinet and keep it next to your bed—it takes up less space—till the child is older.

5. Baby Bedding: Get a mattress, some soft pillows, cotton blankets and sheets for the baby. Don't give him your old sheets. Preferably pre-wash all this bedding in hot water with Dettol or baby clothes' disinfectant and iron it nicely. Change the linen every 5 days or sooner if it gets wet. It's best to keep two sets of bedding handy.

6. **Groovy Gadgets:** Children respond to music and can sleep better when they hear a familiar melody. Get a small music system with a CD changer or iPod, so you can play music for your child in the nursery. Get a baby monitor, so you can sleep comfortably in another room and still hear your child.

7. **Books and Toys:** Certain toys that make rattling sounds and keep your child occupied should be kept on a shelf or in a hamper where it's easy to access them as soon as she starts crying. Later, the shelf can be used to store a few books if you choose to read to your child. It's a very soothing way to make her go to sleep.

8. **Humidifier:** Sometimes, the baby gets a cold or a cough. A humidifier in the room prevents the air in the room from getting too dry and the baby's chest from getting congested. Some humidifiers also have this humming sound that helps babies sleep for longer.

9. **Soft Lighting:** Make sure there are some lamps in the nursery so that when you're putting your child to bed, you don't have to have overhead lighting or, on the other extreme, complete darkness. Keeping a lamp on will help you enter or exit the room easily. It is also reassuring for some kids.

10. **Pictures Aplenty:** Put up photographs of family members, your newborn, smiling children and cartoon characters on the walls or on the shelves to bring happy thoughts into the nursery. A nursery is supposed to be a relaxing place where you bond with your child. Make it special and calming, the way you like it.

Try to have enough space in the nursery to convert it into a child's den when she grows older. The crib will be replaced by a special bed for the child when she is tall and old enough to sleep in it. The changing table can be replaced by a small desk where she can colour or do her puzzles. The floor can have an alphabet rubber mat that you find in most stores so even if the child falls once she starts walking, she won't hurt herself. Be creative with your space. Don't worry if you've converted your guest room into a nursery. A child needs a space to live and play in and guests will understand if you ask them to sleep elsewhere!

You don't have to spend a bomb on doing up the nursery. You can find ways to stick to a budget and yet be creative. Buy some plain cloth and get it dyed to make it into curtains to match your colour palette. Get a second-hand crib, or borrow one from your friends or family who will be happy to help, and repaint it in the colour of your nursery theme. Get a carpenter to build you a small shelf on the wall to put books and toys in. Get stickers of cartoon characters from a bookstore and paste them on the walls. Throw in a colourful floor rug and you're done! If you're arty, you can paint on the bookshelf, crib, drawers and cupboards. If you have a metal cupboard in the room, you can place small, cute magnets on it to make it colourful and interesting. You don't need lots of money to make the nursery special. All you need is love and your special touch!

While you can save on some of the major furnishings in the nursery, the one thing you should splurge on is the baby's bedding. Anything that the baby's skin is exposed to must be new, clean and sanitized. I used to soak everything (even the new clothes that came as gifts) in Dettol water before washing it in hot water with a mild detergent and having it ironed so that if it had any germs from the factory, they would all die before any of it touched my baby's skin. I changed the bedding every few days so I had two or three sets for the baby's room.

The Nanny: Have or Have Not?

I was lucky enough to have good nurses when my children were born. I've kept two nannies to look after them—one for each. It's simply because their age gap is 5 years and each nanny can manage only one child. I know many people who don't have a nanny at all and I marvel at how they manage their careers as well as their children. I've kept two nannies also for the safety of my children. I don't want one to be distracted with one child, and not look after the other properly. A nanny also helps manage your children when you have guests over or when you want to go out somewhere with friends, family or work people but cannot take your children along. It's important to be a woman and connect with other people as well; you can't always be only a mother—a fact I have learnt over the years.

Most of my friends have two, even three, children but they don't have nannies. Some don't like the idea of another person around their child and some feel that nannies are too expensive. Everyone has an individual take on this subject, and it's okay to stick to what makes you feel comfortable. Not all of us will land up with a Mary Poppins, so we can't expect the nanny to do more than just manage the child. As mothers, it is very important to understand that we too need to put in the effort to teach our kids the values we hold precious and help them grow the way we want them to.

If you have twins, looking after both by yourself could get tiring for you. It's advisable to have someone then who will look after one child while you care for the other. You will still bond with both your kids. There is no child in the world who loves his nanny more than the mother who has looked after him.

Affirmation

I'm not going to stress about the small things.
I'm going to enjoy the rest of my pregnancy
and prepare to bring my baby home.

The Birthing Process

Some hospitals and nursing homes allow you to see the operation theatre before your surgery. I checked out the stirrups. I touched them. I saw how wide they go. I asked how many people were going to be there, how many men, how many nurses, how it would happen, who would see me . . . And when they told me, I was just mortified. No, I wasn't scared of the pain. I was more scared of the people looking at me. You may find it funny but, really, I've asked relatives and friends how they did it: 'How did you let your doctor *see* you?'

Well, finally the 9 months were over and it seemed like the longest 9 months of my life. When I went for my final check-up in the last few weeks, I was mentally prepared for a natural delivery and walking out of the clinic in a few hours. But then the doctor told me that the umbilical cord was wrapped around the baby's neck. I didn't know what that meant. What it meant was that the oxygen supply going to the baby was slowly being cut off and they needed to do a caesarean section at the earliest. A part of me was very disheartened as I'd always felt that the whole labour process would have made me more connected to my child. So I went back home and spoke about it to my family who agreed that I must get admitted immediately and get the surgery done.

Now, I can safely say that there is no such thing as bonding better because of the labour process. It doesn't matter how you give birth. As long as the baby is healthy, you will be connected to the baby. The process of giving birth is chosen because of the safety issue. I gave birth both times by C-section at Breach Candy Hospital in Mumbai. The room was beautiful and very clean. The new maternity wing had just been inaugurated and everything was so fresh and sanitary. No flowers were allowed since the pollen could irritate both mother and child but I didn't care. I was just so happy to be with my baby.

When they asked me what music I'd like them to play in the operation theatre, pat I answered, 'Bollywood music!' The doctor looked at me and said, 'Really? Not bhajans or anything devotional?' I said, 'Why? Do you think you need a little more divine power to assist you? No? Cool then, Bollywood music it is!'

Throughout the delivery, it was a relaxed experience, with the doctors joking around and because they had put up a sheet as a curtain for me, I couldn't see anything at all. I kept saying, 'Funny joke, guys, but really, what's happening? What's going on down there?' I couldn't wait for it to be over so I could see my baby, touch my baby . . .

The most amazing feeling in the world is when they put your baby on your breast and you see how completely innocent and how totally wonderful he is. People say that the most amazing things in life are the ones you acquire through travel or vacations or money or as gifts, but I tell you, the moment you see your child for the first time is the most precious gift you can ever give yourself.

Delivery DIY: All the Stuff You Should Do Already

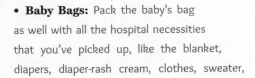

• **Pack It In:** Pack your bag for the hospital well in advance. Put in comfortable pyjamas, bright shirts that open down the front, comfy slippers for padding about, shoes to walk out of the hospital in, a light shawl, hairbrush, toiletries, a nice outfit for when you'll leave the hospital, and anything else you think you may need, a book perhaps, your favourite CDs, your iPad or iPod.

• **Baby Bags:** Pack the baby's bag as well with all the hospital necessities that you've picked up, like the blanket, diapers, diaper-rash cream, clothes, sweater, cap, booties, mittens, onesies, perhaps a soft toy, and whatever else your doctor recommends.

• **Face Time:** Oh, you must take along a basic make-up kit. Tonnes of photos will be taken with you and the baby, and you should look nice. Pack in a little blush, kajal and gloss.

• **Family Fun:** Do not panic if everyone lands up. It's just as exciting for the whole family! Don't start yelling and screaming about why they're there. They hardly care about you—they just want to see the kid you're carrying!

• **File Frenzy:** You must carry your pregnancy file when you go to the hospital, so it's better to tuck it into the hospital bag beforehand lest you forget it in the panic later. The doctor will need to check on certain notes made during your 9 months. If there are critical things that you're allergic to or if you've got a stitch put in or if you're very sensitive to a certain instrument, it will be noted in your file. You won't remember any of these details because you'll be anxious to see your child and nothing else. The doctor won't remember either since they see 400 patients in a day! So carry your file.

• **Razor-Sharp:** Don't be shocked when a nurse comes to shave you. It happens in C-sections. They are not turned on by it! And you don't need to be embarrassed. It's a cleaner and healthier way to deliver a child—and that's far more important than your dignity right now!

• **Delivery Duo:** If you're having a natural delivery, take your partner along to help you with the breathing exercises. Right now you may think that you can inhale and exhale pretty well but wait till the contractions come—you won't remember your bottom from your nostril! A birthing partner really helps in such a situation. Taking classes with him earlier helps even more.

• **What? Me, Shy?** Don't get embarrassed. Just don't. The staff has seen it all before, several times over. Whether you pee inadvertently, whether you scream at your husband, whether you just yell your lungs out—it's natural and they won't care. However, doing it for the dramatics is not cool so keep your personal issues out if you're just mad at your hubby for siding with his mum over something in the distant past!

• **Take Your Time:** You don't need to be a mother as soon as you give birth. The purpose of being in a hospital is that there will be nurses who can look after the baby while you recuperate. So relax, sleep as much as you can, and enjoy the pampering as much as you enjoy the baby.

My entire family was there after both my deliveries and I was glad that the doctor put me out for a few hours because I just didn't want to see anyone right after I'd given birth. A part of me was extremely relieved that the baby was out of me and now there would be other people to help me look after her. Pregnancy is a huge responsibility for a woman. Giving birth is never easy. But the sheer joy you get from smelling your baby close to you for the first time, that joy takes away from any other feeling of doubt you've had all along.

Natural or Caesarean?

This is a question that plagues most pregnant women. Here are the pros and cons of both the basic birthing processes—natural and caesarean—to help you make up your mind.

Yay to a Caesarean

• It is a medical operation. It is done under anaesthesia and there is minimal pain during the process. Many women are frightened of the pain and that fear causes stress during delivery.

• You can schedule it into your calendar. You can pick the best date astrologically or you can plan to have your baby through C-section on such a date that gives you maximum time to recover and bond with the baby after the delivery.

• It is quicker than most labours. The baby's out within minutes, after which they stitch you up. It takes 15–30 minutes for the whole process.

• It helps the baby avoid the journey through the birth canal and any associated risks. This also means that the birthing canal has to do very little work later to get back into shape.

• It is clean. The antiseptic nature of the operation is very different from the physical exertion of labour. In a natural delivery, you will be sweating and possibly peeing too, because the baby presses on your bladder as it pushes its way out.

• It is clinical. There will be no probing of the vagina, which is routine in a normal birth.

• Some women experience lighter postnatal bleeding (lochia) after a C-section.

Nay to a Caesarean

• You cannot jump off the operating table and get right back to your normal life after a C-section. After a natural delivery, you can walk around within a few hours and resume your fitness schedule within weeks. But most women prefer the comfort of a hospital, clinic or nursing home.

• The surgery itself may be completely pain-free but the post-operative recovery period is painful and tiring. There is, of course, a range of painkillers to help mothers through the first few days but, even so, moving around, handling the baby, and using the toilet, all present their own difficulties and have to be tackled slowly and carefully.

• You need to handle your stitches very carefully. There is danger of their getting infected. If they do, you will need more care and may end up back in hospital for a bit.

• You are more flatulent after a C-section. Post-surgery wind may cause discomfort in the abdomen and elsewhere in the body, even the shoulders at times, due to pockets of trapped air.

• You will have a scar, usually a horizontal cut of 5–6 inches, just below the pubic hairline. Though it cannot be seen above a panty, it is a permanent reminder of the surgery.

• You will be asked not to lift weights or do any intensive exercises or even drive for at least 3 months after a C-section. After a natural delivery, you can start your workout within weeks and lose the pregnancy weight quicker.

• You should not lift your older child till your stitches heal. This may cause the older child much angst. Why can Mama lift the baby but not me? Be prepared to answer this question.

• The recovery period is longer as you need to wait for the stitches to heal.

Yay to a Vaginal Birth

• You can have a natural delivery at home if you want to. You don't need to go to a clinic and be in unfamiliar surroundings.

• You will be rushed to the hospital only when the contractions are 5 minutes apart, and you can be at home till then, doing whatever you want to do or just resting.

• Your family is more involved in a natural birthing process. If you have older children, they will see how you brought them into the world and understand the little one better.

• If you are in too much pain, you can take an epidural to cut off sensation in your pelvic area and lower limbs. This reduces the pain by almost 60 per cent and then it's not that bad. Instead of intense pain, you only feel discomfort in pushing the baby out.

• As I said already, after a natural delivery, you can resume your normal lifestyle and your workout regimen within weeks and thus lose all the pregnancy weight real quick. Your body springs back into shape that much faster but you may experience heavier postnatal bleeding after a vaginal birth.

Nay to a Vaginal Birth

- So, there will be a bunch of people in the delivery room helping you push the baby out and they will all be able to see your private parts.

- You may have some incontinence, and may pee or even poop while delivering the baby. This is normal and doctors see it all the time.

- It is generally painful. Fear and tension change hormonal states, physically increasing levels of pain, often to a point where women can no longer cope without painkillers or even an epidural.

- You may need an episiotomy to make a slit in the vagina. Your doctor may recommend it if he feels that extensive vaginal tearing is likely or if your baby is in an abnormal position and needs to be delivered quickly. They will first inject a local anaesthetic to numb the area and you won't feel the incision being made or being repaired after the baby's out. But then the very idea of someone taking a knife (or scissors) to any area of the body, especially the vagina, is a terrifying prospect for any woman! Take heart in the fact, though, that an episiotomy will heal better than a natural tear.

Baby's Breath

Babies born vaginally have a lower risk of respiratory problems. It is widely accepted that the contractions of labour help prepare the baby's lungs to breathe in air. Babies born through a C-section have a higher risk of infant respiratory distress syndrome (IRDS) than babies born vaginally at the same gestational age. In fact, adults with asthma are more likely to have been delivered by caesarean section as compared to adults without asthma.

If you can have it, a normal, straightforward, intervention-free, healthy and natural birth is still the safest, most practical and most advantageous way for a baby to be born. When the birth has gone well, the baby is peaceful, quiet and relaxed. When the birth has gone well, the mother feels stronger, both physically and emotionally. There is a wonderful sense of achievement and peace, of strength and control, of health and completeness, of being able to cope and get on with life in general. It is a very positive and a tremendously life-changing experience.

Affirmation

I welcome this new addition to my life and I will
do what I can to be a good mother—because
from now on, the most awesome moments in life
will always be unplanned and unexpected!

Baby Care, Mommy Care

After my first child was born, I would hold her and cry for hours, worrying that I might break her. Then I would put her down and cry some more, fretting that I was a bad mother for not holding her enough. Then I would be paranoid and ask my mother if I was doing this right or that wrong and what if something happened to her and what if . . . Till my mother would shout at me, 'You're not the first mother in the world, Lolo! Take it easy!' And then I would cry some more!

The most amazing feeling in the world is being alone in a room with your child for the very first time. It's this incredible feeling that the tiny heartbeat has become this 15-inch human being that you've made through all your hard work. Yes, it has taken hard work. Give yourself credit, woman! You ate correctly, you looked after yourself, you stayed calm, you planned things well and you nourished your child superbly in your womb. Half your job is already done, so bravo! You deserve applause for bringing this beautiful, beautiful thing into the world.

Take Your Time

You need to enjoy your baby, your motherhood, your new life . . . So, the most important postnatal-care tip I will give you is that you must advise people not to visit you for the first 2–3 weeks after the delivery. Or you can tell your sister or another close relative to inform everyone. I seriously wish friends and family would just leave the mother alone after she's delivered so she can get a hang of her life before they come barging in to congratulate her or hold her child. A polite way of doing it is putting it up as your BBM or Facebook status. Say that you feel the blessings but you would really appreciate it if people called instead of coming over. Let them know how exhausted you are with the new child and request them to appreciate that you need the space.

After 2–3 weeks, and you feel like having visitors over, you can tell them to come around the time you're most likely to be awake. For most mothers, between 4 p.m. and 6 p.m. is a good window for visits. You can serve some tea and chat for a bit, and still have time for a short rest before dinner time.

Of course, there is always the chance that you will have the entire family descend on you since most Indian families think that they're not 'imposing' but giving their blessings to the child.

Post-partum depression hits most mothers. There are a lucky few who don't get it at all. It is overwhelming to look after a little baby who is completely dependent on you for nutrition, care and love. I was extremely emotional post the births of both my children. I would recommend that you talk to your doctor or family members to ease you out of any mood swings.

Get Out, Get About

I remember the first time I stepped out for lunch after I had Kiaan. I went to Olive in Bandra and I took Samaira along. I was very conscious about my big belly since I hadn't started exercising yet. Wearing pregnancy clothes even after you've delivered can be rather depressing but I realized later that it takes time to heal and get the weight off. You have to realize you're a mom and you should be proud of that. Your weight is not just because you've hogged buffets for the last 9 months. It's because you were nourishing your child, a human being who you've *just* brought into the world. Give yourself time to heal, and in the meantime go out and have fun!

Booby Traps!

After Kiaan, I had a breast abscess and it was excruciatingly painful. You need to massage your breasts regularly and pump out any extra milk if you cannot breastfeed for some time (say, if you go out to work and cannot be back in time). Also, you must rub desi ghee into your nipples so that they don't dry up and get chapped. You can also have frequent warm showers and put a warm-water bottle or heat pads to your breasts to reduce the pain, if any. Within a few days of developing the abscess, I couldn't breastfeed at all. If for some reason, you need to stop breastfeeding (say, you need to take medication that is not contraindicated for breastfeeding), that too can be a problem because the milk won't stop coming till it completely dries up. Be alert about feed timings, be regular with your breast massages and moisturizing, be brainy about your boobs!

Mollycoddling Mama: Ten Tips on Postnatal Mommy Care

1. **Mood Swings:** If you've got the blues or can't sleep well, consult your doctor on what to take or whom to talk to about post-partum depression. Speak to a friend or close relative to relieve your stress. Most important, don't be too hard on yourself if you can't manage the baby too well to start with. It happens, accept it.

2. **Slumber Party:** Sleep as much as you can. You don't need to complete any assignments at this time. And the more you sleep, the better you'll feel and the quicker you'll heal.

3. **Fresh Air:** Go out of the house for fresh air every day. Even if you've had a C-section, walking around your building very slowly or just walking out to sit in the park might help you breathe better.

4. **Diaper Drama:** At night, put your baby in disposable diapers instead of cloth nappies. The baby will sleep better even if he leaks, because the diaper is absorbent. Yes, you need to change it every 3–4 hours for good hygiene but you'll get at least 4 hours of uninterrupted sleep!

5. **Top Feed:** After a while, and if your doctor allows it, you can give your baby top feed (formula) instead of breast milk when you feed him for the last time at night. You

can also give formula to your baby if your doctor thinks that the baby is not getting enough milk from you. Formula is heavier than your milk and flows out easily from the bottle nipple, so the child does not have to work so hard to get it out and has his fill, which makes him sleep longer. The longer he sleeps, the longer you get to rest!

6. **Tiny Treats:** Eat healthy but do indulge in small treats now and then. Overall, you must maintain a healthy diet to keep your milk supply up and to help your body recover completely but if you crave a small piece of chocolate or a bit of mithai now and then, just go ahead. Don't make it a daily indulgence that you might get addicted to (else the kilos won't drop off later) but don't deprive yourself either.

7. **Stay Clean:** Keep yourself clean and hygienic. You may bleed for as long as 20 days after your delivery. Consult your doctor on what products you should use, as regular sanitary napkins might give you a rash. Once your vagina heals, start doing Kegel exercises to strengthen your muscles.

8. **Body Beautiful:** When your doctor allows you to get massages, try and get a relaxing massage once a day. If you don't have the time every day, slot a massage for yourself twice a week, no matter what. A thorough massage will relax all your muscles and also help work off the fat quicker.

9. Tips and Tricks: A friend of mine took 1000 mg of calcium and 500 mcg of magnesium as soon as the baby was born and didn't feel any afterbirth pains. She was wise! Look out for such tried-and-tested tricks and try them, after consulting your doctor of course.

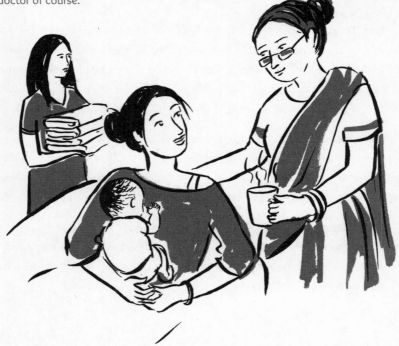

10. Help at Hand: Ask for help. Your parents, husband, family members, friends and maids may not know how or when to help. You need to tell them. Let someone do the laundry, pay your bills, bring your groceries and deal with the daily domestic activities that you don't have time for. You can even tell them to rock your baby to sleep or get you specific toys or clothes that you may have kept on hold in a shop before the delivery or even play with your child while you catch a nap. Don't think you can do it all on your own. Your body and mind will thank you for delegating work instead of trying to be supermom!

Sibling Rivalry

Samaira was born on 11 March, a week before her due date. With Kiaan, I opted for a caesarean on 12 March so I could celebrate their birthdays together for the rest of their lives. So, I had a birthday party for Samaira on 11 March, after which I rechecked my bags and got admitted into hospital on the morning of 12 March. I didn't want Samaira to feel that her mama was pregnant and wouldn't be there for her. I wanted her to have a fun-filled birthday instead of a half-baked party, so I organized a princess-and-tiara theme party and invited all her friends. It was exhilarating but exhausting as well. When Kiaan was born, I told Samaira that this was the biggest gift I was giving her. I had tears in my eyes when she came to see Kiaan and held him in her arms for the first time. I know that will be a significant moment for her for the rest of her life. I was 6 when I went to the hospital and held Bebo in my arms for the first time after she was born. I will never forget that day. At the age of 6, I vowed to always protect her and look after her. I know that Samaira too felt that way about Kiaan. She told me this later.

The Nanny Chronicles

I came back home after just 2 days instead of staying longer in the hospital because I thought I was supermom and had to look after both my older kid and the newborn all by myself. I bounced back pretty quickly but the pain lingered for some time.

Thankfully, I already had a nurse when I brought Kiaan home. Samaira had her maid and I re-employed the nurse who had looked after her when she was born, for Kiaan. It was important for me to get a trained person who could not only look after the baby but also understood hygiene well. So I had a nurse who could sterilize bottles, check the temperature of the water when I was bathing the child, wash all baby clothes in detergent and Dettol water and so on. That extra bit of detailing was very important to me and it helped me tremendously.

Maid to Order

- **Agency Maids:** Find an agency that specializes in maids for newborns. (Always scrutinize the agency's credentials and keep all paperwork with you.) Ask them to shortlist a few candidates whom you can interview. Retain a maid at least a month before the baby is born so that she too is well settled into your domestic life and can help you later. You can gauge her nature and remove her if you don't like her. You don't want to hire someone just when the baby comes because then she too will need to settle in and figure out where things are kept and so on, and you will only get agitated trying to explain things to her when you don't have time in any case!

• **Nurse Natter:** Keeping a nurse might be more expensive but it is worth the money for the first 3–6 months after the baby arrives. She is medically trained and will be able to help you with medicines, clinic appointments and so forth. If you do choose to retain a nurse, do check on her hygiene, qualifications and recommendations.

• **Tick-Tock:** It's not easy to find a full-time maid but I found one for both my children. I found that women who had a 12-hour maid had many issues. She may have excuses for not showing up for work and then you'll be in a fix. You won't know which water she uses to wash her clothes, what her personal-hygiene standards are . . . With a full-time maid who lives with you, you can monitor all these things and make sure she doesn't fall ill or get her treated properly if she does. You must have her undergo a medical check-up before hiring her.

• **Skill Set:** Whether you have a fully literate maid who can read your child to sleep or explain the Universe's problems to him will not matter in the beginning. The child just needs to be fed, bathed, occasionally kept occupied with a rattle, and put to bed. You can tell your family members to read him a story whenever they come and you can sing him to sleep. You don't have to have an educated maid. If she's clean and does her work well, keep her!

• **Money Matters:** Any maid will ask for regular holidays. In Mumbai, there is an agency that provides Bengali maids who will do everything but will take an entire month off every year to go to their villages. You will need to pay for their travel and give them the full month's salary as well. A friend of mine refused to yield to such demands and kept a 12-hour maid. The maid ran away after 8 months for a holiday anyway! There is no guarantee that a maid will stick on. For a few extra hundred or thousand rupees, keep someone reliable till you get the hang of it. And again, if she's come through an agency, you can ask them for a temporary replacement.

Snooze Button

I was fortunate enough to have a separate room for Samaira by the time Kiaan was born. The sleep patterns of *both* the kids will affect you if you're a mother of two, and of all the kids indeed if you have more than two! Now that Kiaan is older, he and Samaira sleep in separate rooms. Earlier, he would sleep with me since Samaira had to wake up early for school every day. I was never forceful with my kids about setting a pattern for feeding, sleeping and playing. I let them find their own groove. With Samaira, I didn't sleep through the night for 2½ years and with Kiaan for a whole year. In spite of having a full-time nanny to help me look after him, I would keep a baby monitor in my room to see if he was sleeping properly, and even despite that I would peep into his room every few hours to check if he was doing okay at night.

I had made up a song I'd sing to Samaira. It was our special song. She used to go to sleep listening to that song. When Kiaan was born, I tried singing that same song to him but Samaira became very possessive, and felt that it was her song alone. I let it be. I sang something else to Kiaan and kept the first song as Samaira's and my special song forever.

Many societies use the Ferber method for making kids sleep. They leave the kid to sleep in his own room for some time, go back after a while and reassure the child that he is not all alone, and then again leave him till he gets used to the fact that he needs to sleep alone. I know many parents who have done this when the kid was 6 months old and have benefited by setting their routines very early on. I was never in favour of this for either of my children. I thought it was too cruel. I was a paranoid mother who wanted her kids to sleep next to her till they were ready to sleep on their own. In our culture, we have the added advantage of family, ayahs, nurses and non-working mothers who can ease the child into a sleeping pattern. Samaira still crawls into bed with me at times and she's 7. But Kiaan has been sleeping alone in his room (with a maid, of course) right from his first birthday. He comes and sees me in the morning when he wakes up. So both the kids have their own growing pattern and I let them be. The less you pressurize children, the better human beings they grow up to be!

Child's Play: Ten Tips on Baby Care

1. **Don't Rock the Walk:** I used to rock Samaira to sleep for 3 years and my back got completely ruined because of it. I never did it with Kiaan and he still slept. The mollycoddling method of rocking or taking a child out for long drives to make him sleep is going to affect you in the long run. Get a chair or put the kid on your lap and rock. Don't hold him and pace the drawing room floor!

2. Get a Car Seat: Put your kid in a car seat from the very beginning. He will fall asleep while strapped to the seat. He will get used to all the belts and buckles and won't make a fuss later on. It's mandatory abroad and it should be followed as a safety rule in India as well.

3. Diaper Dos, Diaper Don'ts: Even though disposable diapers may cost a little more than cloth diapers, don't let your child sit around for hours in a heavy diaper or if he has pooped, don't wait for a few more leaks before you change him. You don't want your baby to get a rash that could cause screaming fits for days for the sake of a few rupees for a diaper change!

4. Swaddle Strategy: Feed the baby, burp the baby, bathe the baby and then swaddle the baby. Wrapping him snugly in a cloth where his hands and feet are cosseted with a fluffy blanket helps him sleep better. He feels he's back in the womb and can sleep for a few hours peacefully.

5. Burp the Baby: After feeding the baby, keep him on your shoulder for at least 15–20 minutes. Even if it's in the middle of the night, you or someone else must hold the baby and make sure he burps before putting him down after a feed. Many babies can choke on their own vomit and it can be fatal. Even if he burps immediately, keep him up for 10 more minutes till all the milk settles down and then lay him back in the crib.

6. Let the Dogs Out: Don't keep stuffed toys in the crib! Many newborns are presented with stuffed toys and dolls, and parents keep all these in the crib or close to where the child sleeps. Keep them away from the child till he's old enough to have a strong immunity. The stuffed toys gather dust and dirt and can cause allergies and harmful diseases.

7. No Tattoo, No Cry: Many cultures/sects believe in piercing the baby's ears or getting the baby tattooed as soon as he is born. I would seriously advise you not to do anything like that till the baby is over a year old, perhaps even wait for longer. He needs to build his immunity first. If the site of a piercing or a tattoo gets infected, it could cause serious harm to an infant who doesn't have the immunity to withstand these dangers. Many cultures also circumcise babies; in this case, please ask your doctor for proper aftercare instructions since a baby boy will need much more attention in the genital area after this procedure.

8. **Babe's Anatomy:** A baby's nails need to be clipped with a soft clipper. When you go for a doctor's visit, ask a nurse to help you clip them. Till then, make him wear soft mittens so he doesn't scratch his face. A baby's genitals need to be cleaned and powdered thoroughly. Rub from top down, not the other way, to avoid infection. When a baby has a cold, you'll need a nose aspirator to pull the mucus out since he won't know how to blow his nose, and keep him elevated with a pillow in his crib.

9. **Child's Play:** Always support your baby's head and neck with your hand. Never play rough. Don't rock him violently or say that he's a 'toughie' who can manage it. He's a newborn and his brain and other body parts are still developing, still very fragile. Be gentle and caring while playing with your child.

10. **Water Babies:** You should give your baby a sponge bath till the umbilical cord falls off and the navel heals completely. In the first year, bathing him twice or thrice a week, or once a day, is sufficient. More frequent bathing may dry up the skin.

Bath Basics

You'll need the following items to bathe your baby:

- A bathing chair: This is a good option for babies under 9 months
- Soft washcloth
- Mild, unscented baby soap and shampoo
- Soft brush to stimulate the baby's scalp
- Towels or blankets
- Infant tub with 2–3 inches of warm—not hot!—water: An infant tub is a baby-sized plastic tub that can fit into your regular bathtub. To test the water temperature, feel the water with the inside of your elbow or wrist
- Clean diaper for later
- Fresh clothes
- Moisturizer for after bath

Sponge Baths: Pick a warm room and a flat surface, such as a changing table, counter or the floor. Undress your baby. Wipe his eyes with a clean washcloth dampened with water only, wiping from the inner corner to the outer. Clean your baby's nose and ears with a clean patch of the same washcloth. Wet the cloth again, add a little soap and wash the baby's face gently and pat it dry. Next, using baby shampoo, create lather, gently wash your baby's head and rinse. Using a wet cloth and soap, gently wash the rest of the baby's body, paying special attention to the creases under the arms, behind the ears, around the neck and in the genital area. Once you have washed these parts, make sure they are nice and dry and then moisturize, diaper and dress your baby.

Tub Baths: When your baby is ready for tub baths, start with gentle and brief baths. If he gets upset, go back to sponging for a week or two, then try again. Undress your baby and place him in the water immediately, in a warm room, to prevent chills. Make sure the water in the tub is no more than 2–3 inches deep, and that water is no longer running into the tub. Use one hand to support the head and the other to guide the baby in, feet first. Speaking to her gently, slowly lower your baby up to her chest into the tub. Use a washcloth to wash her face and hair. Gently massage her scalp with the pads of your fingers or a soft hairbrush, including the area over the fontanelle. When you rinse the soap or shampoo from your baby's head, cup your hand across the forehead so the suds run towards the sides and soap doesn't get into her eyes. Gently wash the rest of her body with water and a little bit of soap. Throughout the bath, pour water gently over her body so she doesn't get cold.

After the bath, wrap her in a towel immediately, making sure to cover her head. Baby towels with hoods are great for keeping a freshly washed baby warm.

Never ever leave the baby alone in the bath! Beware, babies can drown in the littlest of water! If you need to leave the bathroom, wrap the baby in a towel and take her along.

I wanted to be a hands-on mother so I put my career on hold till both my kids were grown-up enough for me to leave them alone with the maids and a family member. I always have a family member around at home when I'm off for a shoot or some event. It's not just about trusting the maids—I feel a family member gives more guidance and can manage situations better if ever there is a crisis. When a mother goes out, she's constantly fretting about whether the child has eaten properly or slept on time or been glued to the TV! With a family member, you don't have any such issues since they'll look after those things.

The reason I finally got back to work in a movie (*Dangerous Ishhq*) was that I wanted to show my children what I did. There was never any pressure to go back to being in the limelight and never any pressure to look good. I have always been a secure person about my looks and what I do. But being a working mom is important, I think. You get that time away from your children to realize your own potential and you can prove to your kids that you're more than just a mom to them. Giving attention to my children in the initial years was very important to me because I'd seen my mother do the same with Bebo and me. Till today, I am a hands-on mother.

Affirmation
I need time to heal.
I will do my best. Beyond that,
I will let the Universe help me.

Eat, Pray, Love, But Do Your Cardio!

Of Binges and Diets, of Baby Fat and the Plié Squat

I'm Not Fat, I'm Pregnant: The Pregnancy Diet

'Congrats, Lolo, you're pregnant!' said my doctor. Of course, I already knew this because I had taken five tests to confirm it at home! But to hear it from my doctor just sent me over the moon.

'Yippee!' I thought. 'I can finally eat for two!' My Punjabi genes took over and I felt as if I needed a dal makhani with butter chicken right then, right there. I'd been watching my weight ever since I got into the movies. That was when I was 16 years old. And although my metabolism had been good enough to help me while I was younger, it had become tougher in recent times (even before I got pregnant) to knock off the kilos. With this news, it felt as if I had been given free rein to eat as I liked.

And so, I ate a piece of chocolate cake every day. Yes, every day. I know this is not advisable but I let myself enjoy every craving I had, even if it was fattening!

Instead of putting on the regular 12–14 kg, I put on 24 kg in my first pregnancy. And trust me, losing 24 kg is far tougher than losing 12 kg. But I never cared for the weight while I was pregnant. I was pregnant—I wasn't fat!

When I went back to my doctor for a check-up, he saw how bloated I was and asked, 'Do you have a water retention problem?' I shook my head solemnly and replied, 'I don't know. Does chocolate cake cause it?' That's when I realized that you don't need to eat for two. Yes, you may be carrying a living being inside you but it isn't the Hulk! You only need to eat 200–500 calories more every day, depending on the trimester you are in. That's just a little more than what you generally eat.

Just Two Happy

I also began to believe that if I was happy, my baby would be happy. So I ate the things that made me happy. Soon enough, like all mothers, I got hold of *What to Expect When You're Expecting* and a few more books on pregnancy and started following them to the T. I believed that what you eat goes into the development of the baby. Then I got obsessed. I ate good food made at home. I'm all for giving in to your cravings as long as you do it at home. If I felt like having Chinese, I would have my cook stir up some dishes without ajinomoto (monosodium glutamate or MSG) in my own kitchen. When I craved pasta, my mother would come over with a penne arrabbiata she'd made. I restricted eating out, not because someone told me to do so but because I knew that if I fell ill, I'd be making my child sick as well. And I never wanted that. So street food like bhelpuri, chaat, and all other *chatpata* things were strictly forbidden.

When you're pregnant, you need to give a year of your life to becoming aware of what you put into your mouth. This is something you will do for your baby. A whole year—9 months of the baby being inside and getting nourishment from you and at least 3 months while the baby is solely dependent on breast milk. (By the way, I think breastfeeding is the most important thing you can do to regain that hot pre-baby figure, but I'll come to that later.) Think about it. If you eat food that is adulterated, would it be healthy? That's exactly what I thought as well when I was nurturing my kids.

Many people don't know this about me but I used to suffer from horrible migraines when I was pregnant. It wasn't just a heatstroke or a headache from all the running around I did—it was terrible migraine. But I decided that I wasn't going to pop that painkiller and make it go away even though my doctor said there were some medicines that would not harm the baby. In my mind, I used to think, 'What if they don't know? What if this pill does harm my baby and they find out only later when they do a study on it? How does it matter if I'm suffering now as long as my baby is okay later?' And so I would sit with a hot or cold compress, apply some balm and not think about the migraine and it would go away eventually. I was that particular about what I put into my mouth. I gave up coffee and all caffeinated and aerated drinks.

And yet, the most important thing was that I never deprived myself of anything. If I felt like eating something, I had it. I just made sure it was made in a clean environment and the ingredients wouldn't harm the baby or me.

Maternity Munches: The Most Important Foods during Pregnancy

- **Milk, Lots:** Have five glasses of milk. Yes. The baby needs calcium. I would have five servings of milk in the form of paneer, yogurt, cheese, small doses of ice cream or simply milk.

- **Veggies, Lots:** Grilled vegetables, steamed vegetables and stir-fried vegetables in great quantities keep your tummy happy. Red and yellow bell peppers are great. Get some spinach home and make a soup or palak paneer. Surprisingly, I craved broccoli. So I had tonnes of it and now both my children love broccoli!

• **Protein Punch:** I'm a chicken eater. But when I got pregnant, I really did not feel like eating chicken. So I had proteins in the form of the right type of fish, paneer and dal. Some types of fishes out there are not good for babies and you should avoid them. Check with your doctor first. But dals are the best thing you can have as well as chickpeas (chholey) and kidney beans (rajma).

• **Fruit Basket:** Two servings of fruit a day are important. Not papaya or pineapple though. Fruit and veggies give you fibre and that helps prevent constipation. Avoid juices, however, even later when you're trying to lose all the weight. Instead, eat a bowl of whole fruit.

• **Water Babies:** I have eight glasses of water a day in any case, but I started drinking more when I was carrying. Having loads of water really helps. It flushes out toxins, keeps you hydrated, and balances your body. Initially I didn't have so much water thinking that it was cold so I didn't need to. But once I consciously started drinking ten glasses a day, I could see how it helped me. You know, that pregnancy glow is mostly due to water!

• **Nutty Nuggets:** Almonds are a great form of nutrition for you and your child. And walnuts . . . Omega 3 baby! Need I say more?

• **Ande ka Funda:** An egg a day gives you your required protein and omega 3 fatty acids which help develop the baby's brain.

• **Whole Grains:** You can have a bowl of popcorn every day, as long as it's not artificially flavoured or extra buttery, because it adds fibre to your system. Plus, it's easy to munch when you're bored at home. Other whole grains, like oatmeal with a little bit of milk, can make a great snack.

- **Yay Yogurt:** Yogurt made at home is great not only as a source of calcium but also as a precaution to keep infections at bay. Good, good, good! A katori of yogurt with a dash of sugar would keep me going for a couple of hours.

Pregnancy is guilt-free eating time. It gives you the funniest cravings that you will always remember. This friend of mine craved the weird combination of peanut butter and pickle! I had my slice of chocolate cake every day. Some may want rich fudge ice cream in the middle of the night. I say go for it! Enjoy it all as long as you can hold it down. So I had my share of chips, French fries, cakes and pizzas. I loved my junk food as much as my healthy food. I wasn't eating healthy to avoid piling on the kilos. I hardly cared if I fit into my old jeans or not! I knew I would be determined enough to shed it all later. But pregnancy for me was freedom food time. And yet there were a few things I avoided . . .

Tummy Taboos: Foods to Avoid during Pregnancy

- **Coffee/Tea:** Caffeine is generally not good for the baby. But if you have a craving for it, then have it very rarely. I love my coffee and lemon tea. But I totally gave them up both times.

- **Aerated Drinks:** I have a can of Diet Coke every day but, during my pregnancy, I gave that up along with other regular sodas and colas.

- **Liquor:** A big no-no! It can do so much damage to your child that you will regret it later.

- **Chinese Food:** I love Chinese food but I realized that the MSG they use in many eateries can harm my child. So I gave it up completely. Also, it was strange that I didn't crave it. If you must have it, stick to rice and noodles but avoid the dim sum, the sauces and the fried stuff.

- **Raw Food:** Salads, coleslaw, relishes and other forms of raw food like sushi are best avoided. You don't know how well they have been cleaned and what substances have gone into making them edible.

- **Fish with Mercury:** Certain fish (including shellfish like prawns) with mercury are better left untouched during pregnancy. You never know how fresh or stale they are.

- **Papaya and Pineapple:** Keep away from these two fruits, even their juices. They cause heat in the body and it is known that in the olden times they were given to induce contractions.

- **Unpasteurized Cheeses:** Don't have blue-veined cheeses or any cheese that is aged and matured.

- **Organ Meat:** Avoid liver and its derivatives like pâté. Too much vitamin A is not good. You may love making kaleji at home but it's not the best form of iron to have when you're expecting. Have iron supplements instead.

- **Cold Cuts and Mayonnaise:** Salami, ham slices, pepperoni, fish (like salmon gravlax) and other frozen foods that you generally put in sandwiches and on subs should be avoided. Mayonnaise is made from egg, and can also be quite harmful.

Most women feel very sick during their pregnancies and can't even think about food. Luckily, I didn't have too much of the morning sickness—just the usual 3 months with Samaira and 4 with Kiaan. A friend of mine had morning sickness for 5 whole months! So while I was eating my cheese sandwich, she would look at me like she wanted to kill me because she wasn't able to hold anything down. I gave her a very light diet, things that her body could absorb, like soup, toast with jam, lightly sautéed vegetables, dals, lemon tea, crunchy cereals and light milk. I had to keep the aroma light so it wouldn't overpower her. It was a hit-or-miss situation.

It's also a question of environment. Perhaps your household is used to making and eating a certain type of food. At times, however, our bodies crave something lighter, something sweeter or just something different. That's when we can try cuisines from other regions, like idlis or poha or a very light dosa. If you're used to having puris and jalebis every morning, why not try some cereal with milk instead? Experiment at home and see what suits you. Get enough nourishment and always consult your doctor when you feel you're not getting enough food into your body. The doc may give you a few more calcium or vitamin tablets to compensate for the nutrition you may be missing until you can eat again. And don't worry, eating or not, you're doing it all for your baby and the Universe is going to help you!

Alimentary, My Dear Watson

Here are some other dietary and related tips that helped me throughout my pregnancies:

• Eat every 2 hours. I know you're thinking that's some six to seven meals in a day! But try the sample diet plan at the end of this chapter, with your doctor's okay, of course. Eating every 2 hours will prevent the acidity, heartburn and gas you will inevitably have during pregnancy.

• Take your vitamins, calcium and folic acid. Doctors even prescribe folic acid to women who are trying to get pregnant; it's supposedly a miracle drug but don't overdose on it! The right amount could help your baby in ways that no amount of nutrition can. Calcium reinforces your bones to hold all the weight you're gaining. Vitamins, iron and zinc give your body a boost and help your baby grow healthy. Don't skip these. It might feel like many pills but if your doc prescribes 'em, eat 'em!

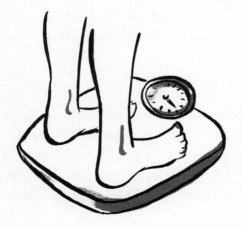

• If you are not in your normal weight range while you're pregnant, your doctor may give you a diet to help accelerate or control your weight gain. Be vigilant about that.

• Whether you cook at home or eat out, be conscious and conscientious about the amount of oil that goes into your food. Indulgence doesn't mean you can eat very oily food.

• Salt causes water retention. If you're used to grabbing the salt shaker and adding that extra amount, stop now.

• Sleep. If you're the type of mom who's always on the go and is working non-stop, now is the time to re-evaluate how much you need to rest. Ideally, you should get 7–8 hours of sleep or even more at night and maybe an hour in the afternoon as well. But if you work in an office and cannot manage that, try to put your feet up after lunch and grab some shuteye, even if it is for 10 minutes. Tell your boss that it rejuvenates you to work harder! Sleep early. Late nights are not recommended. Never push yourself to do something when you're tired. Your health is more important than any work you'll ever do.

• Wash your hands before and after every meal and after you use the loo. If you're averse to so much water and feel that your hands are getting dry, use a hand sanitizer or a moisturizer. But wash your hands as often as possible. Keep a separate towel to wipe your hands and face, a towel just for you. You don't want other people's germs!

• Avoid artificial sweeteners. I've never had artificial sweeteners before, during or after my pregnancy. One teaspoonful of sugar or a bit of gud and honey to sweeten things is fine by me. The chemicals in all these artificial things are not good for you at all and they hardly help in keeping the weight down or getting it off.

• Try not to get tempted by sandwiches, bakery breads, buns, dhoklas, pizzas, pancakes, khaman, steamed rice cakes, tomatoes, tamarind and kadhi as they usually increase your oedema and acidity.

• Do not eat leftovers or deep-frozen foods.

• If possible, avoid fasting during pregnancy. After all, you're doing the best thing in the world by looking after your child. God wants you to look after it well. Say your prayers, but eat!

Diet for Doubles

Rujuta Diwekar has been my dietician for a long time. She seems to be the 'family dietician' for all of us. I think it is because she works for our bodies. You can go to whichever dietician you want during and after your pregnancy. The basic thing is to eat healthy for the baby while you're still breastfeeding and then gradually get stricter when you're weaning and trying to lose weight. The three stages of pregnancy require different amounts of food. In the first 3 months, you can eat lighter; from the third to the sixth month, you may indulge a bit more if your morning sickness has ebbed; and in the last 3 months, you may start being careful with the fatty things since they'll give you heartburn and disturb your sleep. Here is a sample diet that I would recommend while you're pregnant:

8 a.m.

1 bowl of cornflakes and milk

Or

Eggs + toast and jam

Or

Poha

Or

Upma

Or

2 idlis

Or

1 home-made dosa + 1 katori sambar + 1 tsp chutney

10 a.m.

1 bowl of any fruit you like (banana, mango, chicku, apple, etc.)

Noon

1 plate rice/2 rotis + 1 katori dal + 1 katori sabzi + 1 katori dahi

(You can have two pieces of chicken instead of dal or substitute the entire meal with fish curry and rice.)

2–3 p.m.

1 katori dahi + some walnuts + a few almonds + 1 glass nimbu-paani/1 cup herbal tea

(With regard to the nuts: if you're craving sweets, have 1 piece, and if you're craving savouries, have a handful.)

5 p.m.

1 cheese sandwich

Or

1 slice of home-made pizza

Or

A sandwich with lots of veggies and steamed chicken or paneer with salt, pepper and some chaat masala or even a peanut butter and jelly sandwich or some peanut butter with apples

7 p.m.

A soup + pasta/tacos

Or

Home-made Chinese food

Or

Whatever you had for lunch; fish, broccoli, sweet potato, three-bean salad or tofu, a bowl of vegetables, buckwheat noodles, cucumber-and-tomato salad are all good

9 p.m.

Low-fat cheese and pear

Or

A handful of nuts and raisins

Or

Hummus with carrots

Or

Some milk rusks

Or

A simple glass of milk

10 p.m.

Sleep time

You don't have to eat everything all the time. You need to figure out how much your body needs. Don't stuff yourself or you'll get indigestion! Even a little bit of munching will keep your metabolic rate up and allow you to indulge in your cravings. If you must eat out, here are some recommendations.

Dine-Out Dos and Don'ts

- Slice of grilled chicken or turkey breast with lettuce and tomato on a whole-wheat roll
- Two slices of pizza
- Steamed idlis or plain dosas
- Light pastas without heavy, creamy sauces; eat half and pack half for someone else!
- Chicken or seafood stir-fry; ask for 'low oil, low sauces'
- If you're eating north Indian food, take very small portions; all that dal makhani, butter chicken, tandoori naan and paneer malai is filled with just lard!

Affirmation

I will enjoy my food but I will not go overboard.
I will be mindful about what I put into my mouth.
I will be happy with my choices of food today.

Get the Oomph Back: The Post-Pregnancy Diet

The moment I woke up from my caesarean the first time, I promptly looked down at my stomach hoping that it had miraculously gone back to being the washboard it was before pregnancy. Obviously, I was in for a huge disappointment. Stomachs don't automatically shrink just because your baby is out. It takes time and effort to shrink them. Being the highly motivated woman that I am, I asked my doctor when I could start getting back into shape. She said, 'Shut up! You have plenty of time for that.' And she was right. You cannot think of a fitness plan for at least 40 days after a C-section.

What you can think of, indeed must think of, right away, is your nutrition plan. So, the daily dose of chocolate cake stopped the minute I delivered. Even though I felt I'd gone through this earth-shattering experience of giving birth to another human and 'OMG, I so deserved a little treat to celebrate all I'd been through!' I remembered that I *had* celebrated. I had eaten everything I liked for 9 months.

Every day. So why did I need to celebrate now? It was just pushing out a kid, something which millions of women do every day anyway. And just like that, I let go of that chocolate cake. And all the goodies that visitors brought.

I asked my doctor and Rujuta, my nutritionist, what I should eat to give maximum benefit to my child and lose weight in the process. Like me, most women stay at their mom's place after delivery. So, for 40 days, I could command my mother to make whatever I liked. And I refused to eat out or eat food from outside. There is a reason for this. You have just had a baby. You will be in pain. Whether you have had a natural delivery or a caesarean, your body has gone through wear and tear and it needs to heal. Also, your sleep patterns have changed and you are feeling disoriented. To go out to party or dine should be the last thing on your mind. Getting adequate rest and nutrition should be of prime importance.

It was 3 months after Samaira's birth that I went out for the first time, with much angst and guilt about leaving her for 2 hours at night, that too after she had gone to sleep! My mother berated me, saying, 'My God, Lolo, you're not the first mother in the world. Live a little!' I think I barely spoke that evening because my mind kept wandering off to whether my daughter would wake up and need me and that would mean I was a bad mother . . . It's only now that I realize that you can't think like that. It's FINE! Well, I went to my favourite eatery, Olive, while I was pregnant. I never had sushi though, during pregnancy or after the baby. I had lots of steamed vegetables and teriyaki chicken with rice.

So, as I said, while I couldn't start my fitness regimen immediately, I did start with my diet plan.

My Daily Diet after Pregnancy

8 a.m.

Warm water with lemon and honey

8.30 a.m.

Fruit

9 a.m.

Tea, egg, toast

11 a.m.

Poha/peanut butter with toast/soup

1 p.m.

Fish curry with rice

2–3 p.m.

Cheese on toast

Or

A glass of milk

5 p.m.

Tea with a brown-bread sandwich, full of vegetables

Or

Upma

Or

Dahi with fruit

7.30 p.m.

Pasta without cheese

Or

Two rotis + dal + sabzi/chicken/fish

Each pregnancy is different. I had two caesarean procedures, and needed to be very careful after both. I needed to start my day with a good breakfast because I started walking within 45 days and, for that, I needed my energy. For lunch,

I had a lot of fish curry and rice and still lost all my weight. Many people were shocked and said, 'How can you have rice?' I was most adamant though. I believe that you should eat in moderation and it is a myth that rice makes you put on weight. I did consult a dietician and the key thing was to eat regularly and be very particular about timings. I don't believe in the no-carb diet. Carbs are good if eaten correctly.

I have a theory. I think that if you give up carbs, you get cranky. You must include them in your daily diet. Whole-wheat is better than multigrain bread. Now here's the deal. I'm very suspicious of multigrain bread—you don't know how many grains have gone in there and if they *all* suit your system. Also, it sits very heavy in your stomach. A chapati or a whole-wheat toast is a far better option.

Let me reiterate that I didn't eat raw foods even after pregnancy. I'm not too much of a salad person and I'm paranoid about eating raw stuff. Grilled, steamed and stir-fried are all healthy options.

The Milky Way: Breastfeeding and Diet

When I started breastfeeding, my diet also changed. I focused on things that would help me produce milk. I started having fish and methi. I even had the laddoos that Punjabis eat but I made sure they were made with gud.

By the way, breastfeeding makes you lose weight. It has been researched and proven that mothers who breastfeed lose about 550 calories every day! That's like an hour and a half on the treadmill. You can actually feel your stomach muscles contracting back into shape when you breastfeed. But remember that just because you're burning those calories doesn't mean you eat a brownie a day to compensate!

If, for some reason, you can't breastfeed, your calorie restrictions should be more stringent, so check with your doctor as to how much you should eat. Sadly, with Kiaan, I couldn't breastfeed for as long as I wanted to because I developed an abscess on my breasts. I was so heartbroken. Not only could I not give my child the nutritional benefits of mother's milk but my stomach muscles too needed more help to contract, which meant no more yummy gud laddoos!

I am all for breastfeeding. If you can do it, please do it. It's a myth that breastfeeding will make your breasts sag. Boobs sag because of bad bras, not because of a latched-on kid!

Diet Doctor

• Make soup at home. Use different vegetables or chicken and make a nice broth without cornflour. It is healthy and tasty. It helps you lose weight and still gives you nutrition.

• Dahi with fruit is a good alternative to desserts. Mix whatever fruit is at home into the dahi and have it like a sorbet. You can chill it or make a smoothie. It gives you a calcium kick and satisfies your sweet cravings.

• Egg whites are excellent. You can have four, even five, egg whites a day or mix in one yolk. There are hundreds of egg recipes you can try. I used to put mushrooms, spinach and cottage cheese in my omelette and it would become a whole meal. An excellent form of nutrition, it fills your stomach without adding too many calories. It is also an excellent choice when you are eating out.

• Carry food along. If you are going back to work or travelling, there will be long periods when you will not find food anywhere or will have the wrong choices in front of you. You must always carry a fruit and tiffin. Never starve yourself for long periods. Dry fruit, dahi with fruit and even a cheese sandwich are great   options.

I am a huge fan of journals; I think it's important to jot down things. So I used to write down what I ate and where. I could track which food patterns worked for me. I went to restaurants and had cheat days as well. I am a big foodie and I live to eat! But because I did it correctly,

it worked for me. There were days when I would go out and overeat because all my favourite foods were being served. The next day, I would feel enormous guilt and walk extra on the treadmill. If you're good to your body, results will show. But you should never rush it. Be wise with your diet.

Busting Some Diet Myths

When you recognize what your body needs and start eating healthy, you'll never need a diet. You'll never need to give up all the foods you like, nor ever starve yourself. After your child is born, you need to eat very healthy because you will be feeding your baby. All the nutrients your child gets come from your diet. So if you don't eat right, your child suffers. Even after you stop breastfeeding, you must look after yourself. Children need healthy, happy mothers, not undernourished, cranky women in desperate need of vitamins!

Some people are misinformed that they should not eat carbs at night. Well, I have eaten fish curry with rice at night and lost weight. We need to recognize the foods that can help us maintain a healthy figure rather than focus on things that make us 'look' healthy.

Just like you plan your child's daily tiffin, so must you plan your own meals. When you have your diet chalked out, it's easy to stay on track. Once I lost those 24 kg of pregnancy weight, I never put it back on. I eat what I want, when I want to, but always in moderation, and always work it off later. I know you can too. Just believe in yourself. If you really want to be thin, don't be an emotional or social eater—be an intelligent eater!

Please, No Myths in Our Mouths!

- **Dairy Dilemma:** Milk products are excellent for your system. Rustle up a fruit yogurt when you have sweet cravings. Add a spoonful of honey to dahi if you feel peckish between meals. Have cold coffee without sugar or a mango/strawberry shake with half a teaspoon of sugar. Blend skimmed milk, crushed ice and vanilla essence to make a superb summer shake.

- **Sugar Shun:** Two spoons of sugar in a day are fine. Avoid having more than that. I never use sweeteners in my tea or coffee. If you examine your food's sugar content, you'll be surprised to know how many hidden sugars it has. Battle your sweet craving and watch the kilos slide off.

- **Soupy Saga:** I would not advise a soup-and-salad diet unless you need to shed a few stubborn kilos right before an important event. It cannot be a way of life. You'll soon put the weight back on because your body needs regular food.

- **Detox Drama:** Again, a short-term measure, good for undoing holiday excesses. But you cannot live on detox. If I need to cleanse my system, I go on a detox diet but only for a day at the most. And I eat a little less food rather than no food at all.

- **Carb Critique:** Everything has carbs—rice, bread, biscuits, cakes, sugar, dry fruit, crackers, low-fat munchies, jams, pickles, potatoes, lentils, pasta . . . There is no point in giving up carbs, because carbs give us energy. They are lighter on the kidneys than proteins. Good non-fatty sources of carbs are vegetables, oatmeal, brown rice, whole-grain breads, and lentils. If you want to have white rice and pasta, have small bowlfuls rather than giving them up altogether.

- **Coffee Conflict:** I love coffee but I have only one or two cups a day. People think green tea breaks down fat but I'm not a believer. I'm not too fond of the taste either! A couple of glasses of hot water with lemon after every meal really cuts the fat though. Camomile tea relaxes me (during intense shoots) but I prefer drinking water over that or a fizzy drink or coffee. I don't drink black coffee as it dries the skin but, with a squeeze of lemon, it can counter diarrhoea!

- **Meaty Matters:** I love fish and chicken. White meat is rich in protein, which helps our muscles develop. Avoid red meat, as it stresses the kidneys and raises cholesterol levels. It's a myth that you can eat either meat or carbs in one meal. I eat fish curry with rice almost every day. Your body needs a little of everything.

• **Egg Endeavour:** An egg is the healthiest snack for children and mothers everywhere. It's nutritious, low-cal, versatile and great for the heart. If you want to lose weight, avoid the yolk. Take a few egg whites, throw in some veggies and bingo—you have your low-cal meal.

• **Juice Justice:** Having a glass of fruit juice instead of a cola may not be the best strategy! Fruit juices may have higher sugar content than regular colas. If you really want to lose weight, avoid both and sip on chilled water. Squeeze in some lemon and muddle in some mint leaves for a refreshing change.

• **Choco Charm:** Think chocolate gives you acne? You are mistaken. Too much of anything gives you acne. A piece of dark chocolate every alternate day can actually keep your craving for an entire brownie away for far longer than you think. Four pieces of Lindt Dark Chocolate (70 per cent cocoa) have 250 calories and 19 gm of fat. Decide when you really need it and indulge yourself. If you shun all chocolate all week, you are bound to binge on an entire cake over the weekend!

• **Raw Reserves:** Raw food can contain harmful salmonella. If salads are not washed properly, you can fall very ill. Sushi and sashimi (raw fish) can be harmful for pregnant women. Raw protein of any kind—chicken, fish, meat—may have enzymes that you can react badly to. If you're eating a salad, make sure it's fresh and cleaned well. Foods cooked in minimum oil at a low temperature actually retain all the nutrients and are healthy.

• **Lo-Cal Loss:** Diet chips, chiwda, cookies are all myths, whether processed in a different oil or even baked. They still have carbs, sugars, fats! Because they contain negligible calories, you tend to eat far more because you're tricked into thinking they are healthy! I learnt this from my dietician, Rujuta, when I was gorging on diet wafers. If you really want fried food, have a few bites to satisfy your craving.

• **Alcohol Alert:** Alcohol raises the level of good cholesterol, which prevents plaque build-up in the arteries and reduces clotting factors that contribute to heart attacks/ strokes. Any alcoholic beverage consumed in moderation (one to two drinks a day) reduces the risk of heart disease. But, remember, alcohol also contains calories, as do the crunchy munchies that taste so good along with it!

• **Salt Surprise:** I can't believe that people give up salt to lose weight. It doesn't help. If there is no taste in your diet food, you will soon start hating your diet. A teaspoonful of salt while you're blanching your vegetables actually helps retain the nutrients and in cooking them faster. You don't need to add extra salt on top of all the food to make it tastier but the average bit of salt that goes into daily cooking is essential to stay on a healthy diet.

• **Salad Story:** So you've gone out for dinner. You've ordered a salad, as you think it's healthy. Then you get on the scales the next day and realize that you've put on a few hundred grams. Want to know what you did wrong? You put dressing in that salad. A heavy dressing makes the calorie count go up. Take a light vinaigrette dressing on the side and dip your fork into it if you must. That cheesy dip you had with cucumber also adds to the calories. The best option is a low-fat hummus with whole-wheat pita.

• **Broth Brouhaha:** I love people who say they have soups every day but have not seen the kilos roll off. When I ask them what type of soup they have, they say cream of mushroom and cream of chicken. Well, there's your problem. Anything with cream in it will have 200 calories more than clear soups. Soups are also made in oil and when you add butter on top with a few deep-fried croutons, they are very yummy. Don't think you're going to lose weight by having them though. They are great fillers for children who need to have something with vegetables in it but are tired of eating vegetables for real.

• **Sandwiches Self-Help:** 'I had a light lunch—a sandwich and a cappuccino,' said a dear friend, just the other day. And I burst out laughing. There's nothing light about it! A sandwich has bread, mayonnaise, processed meat and a salad leaf. You're fooling yourself if you think it's less than 300 calories. And a cappuccino, which is made with foam and heavy milk, is another 300 calories. Add them up and you'll see that having two chapatis, two pieces of chicken and some vegetables is lighter! If you want to eat a really light sandwich, get some whole-wheat bread and add your own grilled chicken and fresh veggies. That way you can monitor how much you're eating and how good it really is.

Belly Bible: Ten Diet Commandments

1. Eat small amounts, but eat every 2 hours. Keep your metabolic rate up. Avoid both feasting as well as fasting. Don't ever skip meals, don't ever overeat.

2. Don't pair colas, sodas or other drinks with your food. They dilute the nutritional value of the food. And don't drink colas anyway while you're breastfeeding. They will give your kid gas so bad that he'll be crying through the night and you won't get any sleep either. Then you'll really regret it and all I'll say is 'I told you so!'

3.   Avoid caffeine after your lunch. You don't need coffee to stay awake if you've had a light lunch. The caffeine washes away everything healthy. That's my belief.

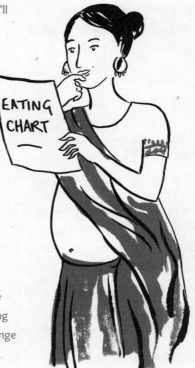

4.   Eat slowly. Even if your baby is crying—and believe me, he will, as soon as you sit down for your meal—get someone to calm him down while you chew your food thoroughly.

5.   Don't stock your kitchen with things that will tempt you. Even if you're having visitors and you want to serve them some snacky stuff, make a poha instead of offering chips and cookies—those will only make you binge when you get up for the 2 a.m. feed. Trust me!

6.   Drink lots and lots of water. If you don't like plain water, add a little lemon and mint to it and have it chilled.

7.   Eating buttered and flavoured popcorn and other such snacks while watching a film is very dangerous. The artificial flavouring, not to mention the numerous calories, are eminently avoidable. No, you don't really need popcorn to enjoy a film!

8.   Italian and Indian foods are good options if you feel like eating out even while you are pregnant, and you can find low-calorie items on the menu for after the baby. A tandoori roti with a few pieces of chicken tikka or paneer tikka should suffice. A whole-wheat pasta arrabbiata with veggies is a tasty dish. Greek food is also a good option since it includes hummus and you can ask for whole-wheat pita bread, grilled vegetables and chicken.

9.   Avoid buffets. There may be food that has been lying there for a very long time.

10.   For air or train travel, carry food from home. I would take a sandwich from home whenever I was flying the Delhi–Bombay sector. Avoid plane or train food. Even though the food might be better for those who travel in higher classes, it is still not as fresh as home-made stuff. And oh, avoid those hot bhajias at stations, thinking they're fresh—they're not; they're reheated God knows how many times, God knows in what oil!

While the best way to lose weight is to eat at home, I understand that you're dying to go out and party a little. Perhaps you want to have a romantic dinner with your husband while your mom looks after your child. Some of the best things to eat at restaurants are given below. Be warned, it will set you back on your diet, so don't indulge in eating out more than twice a week.

Dine-Out Dos and Don'ts

- **Chinese:** Clear soups, stir-fried vegetables or chicken, a bowl of plain rice; no MSG, no extra sauces
- **Italian:** Whole-wheat pasta arrabbiata with veggies or chicken; stay away from the bread basket, the olive oil and the dessert!
- **Indian:** A tandoori roti, chicken/fish/paneer tikka; no iced tea or desserts or dals
- **Food Courts:** A bowl of soup, grilled chicken, idlis
- **Coffee Shops:** A sandwich filled with cooked veggies or chicken (no mayo, no dressing), a cup of coffee or tea with skimmed milk
- **South Indian:** A plain dosa (low oil), a plate of idli/poha; no upma, masala dosa, or uttapams, to cook which you need a lot of oil

Affirmation
I will not starve myself.
It's not good for my baby or me.
I will look haggard and age quicker if I do.
I will eat correctly and show the world
the right way to lose weight.

Body Beautiful: Fitness during and after Pregnancy

Fitness during Pregnancy

I have a confession to make. I did not exercise during my pregnancy.

I know what you're going to say—that it's blasphemous, that one must exercise! But honestly, during my first pregnancy, I was just so happy being pregnant and also so paranoid that I didn't want to take a chance with losing the baby. Now, in hindsight, I know that was silly. My doctor told me to keep doing whatever I was used to doing but I didn't want to listen.

During my second pregnancy, I was more confident about my body and my pregnancy, plus I was already a mother to a 4-year-old school-going child. I was also redecorating our house in Mumbai, looking into every detail. While I dropped and picked Samaira to and from school and monitored her extracurricular activities, I also single-handedly supervised the building and furnishing of the house, which I enjoyed thoroughly.

I kept myself busy. I walked every day, though not on a treadmill. I was not stressed about my pregnancy and did little things around the house to keep myself as active as I could.

I wouldn't recommend that you begin on an exercise plan once you get pregnant. I would suggest that you continue with one if you have been following it for a long time. Please check with your doctor about what you are allowed to do and how much your body can take.

Mom in Training: Working Out during Pregnancy

• Drink plenty of water. You need about three times more than you generally drink. Not drinking enough water can cause cramps.

• Take your calcium, vitamins and folic acid daily. Don't take any tablets to lose weight!

• Have healthy shakes and smoothies instead of whey protein or any such thing with artificial colouring and taste.

• Don't push yourself to stay thin. You are going to put on weight. It's natural and healthy. Don't stress over it.

• Don't stretch your body too much. If you feel dizzy, light-headed or uncomfortable, stop exercising immediately.

• Some yoga asanas may be harmful for the baby. Check with an expert.

• Avoid the stairs and the stepping machine at the gym. Most doctors say so.

• Avoid gymnastics, please! All that tumbling and balancing could go wrong as your centre of gravity shifts with your increasing weight.

• Avoid weights but use your body for freehand exercises.

• Swelling in the legs and feet is a normal, albeit frustrating, part of pregnancy. You can put them up whenever you get a chance; aquatic exercises also help reduce swelling. Check with your doc and go to a clean pool for some exercises.

• Wear correct shoes and clothes to exercise. Walking in chappals is not good for your back.

Speaking of Pelvic Thrusts!

There is one exercise that every woman must do during and after pregnancy. It is called the Kegel exercise. It is a pelvic-floor exercise that strengthens the muscles in your vagina. You need to repeatedly contract and relax the muscles in the pelvic region. It helps tremendously during a natural childbirth, and later, it helps get your vagina back in shape as well as control your bladder.

How do you know if you're doing it correctly? Try to stop the flow when you urinate. If you can, you've got the basic move. Don't make a habit of starting and stopping your urine stream though. Doing Kegel exercises on a full bladder or while emptying your bladder can actually weaken the muscles as well as hinder complete emptying of the bladder, and increase the risk of a urinary tract infection.

Try it four or five times in a row. Work up to keeping the muscles contracted for 10 seconds at a time, relaxing for 10 seconds between contractions. Be careful not to flex the muscles in your abdomen, thighs or buttocks. And don't hold your breath; instead, breathe freely. Do it three times a day.

Fitness Fundas: My Workout Secrets

• **Eat before You Start:** I always eat something before I work out. Even having a rusk before I head for yoga helps my metabolism jump into action. If you're going running, have half an apple, a whole banana or some oatmeal half an hour before you start. Never work out on an empty stomach. It's one of the worst things you can do because you'll soon get dizzy and defeat the purpose!

• **Feel Stylish:** I would tie my hair up so it wouldn't fall on my face. I bought bright workout gear and wore that for my walks. You don't need to look cool for anyone else—you just need to feel slightly stylish for yourself, to keep yourself motivated.

- **Strengthen Your Back:** Before you get pregnant, start your back exercises so you won't have aches and pains when you put on weight. You may need to avoid these exercises while you're pregnant, though, as they involve lying on your stomach.

- **Mind Your Posture:** Stand and sit up straight, shoulders back and chest out. Don't tuck in your tummy when you are pregnant. Correct posture pre-empts aches and pains.

- **Work with Gravity:** As you get bigger and your centre of gravity shifts, you may need to walk slower. Pushing yourself into brisk walking isn't going to help you shed those kilos right now. You need to see where you're going so you don't trip and fall!

The most important advice I'd give to all you mothers-to-be out there is this: don't stress over anything! There are some people who read the newspaper every morning and get depressed. There are some who get annoyed if the plumber doesn't arrive on time. There are some who overthink and over-plan and get very stressed when things don't work as per their plans! Fret not, let it be, just chill . . . Pregnancy is a beautiful time for you to think of nothing. Enjoy your special status. Feel the joy.

I used to sit and surf all the pregnancy sites when I was expecting. I used to wonder if what I ate would harm the baby. If I bent over to pick up a pencil, I'd wonder if I had squished the baby's neck. I was quite paranoid. I would sincerely advise you to stop fretting about the minutiae. If you have a healthy pregnancy, figure out what exercise you like to do and stick to it for as long as you can. If you have a precarious pregnancy, don't worry about exercising. Worrying is not going to help you. Keep your mind active and always be happy.

Even after the baby is born, stick to an exercise you like, be it dancing, Zumba, yoga, Pilates, gymming or running. Exercise is not just for losing weight. It's a great mood enhancer. It gives you a surge of endorphins, which make you feel brighter about life. And if you're suffering from post-partum depression, exercise will alleviate it. Join a class if you think you can't do it alone. You can also ask a friend to come along with you in the beginning to get you started. Track your progress by noting down what you ate and how you felt on any given day. Give yourself time during and after your pregnancy to nurture yourself. Exercise is just one way.

The Power of Yoga

Once I was a gym enthusiast and treadmill trooper. Now, thanks to Bebo, I'm a complete power-yoga person. I don't need to go to the gym or do heavy weight training. My body weight is enough for me to build strength and stay healthy. Yoga has made me spiritually and physically better too. Here are some tips from my experience:

- **Trainer Brainer:** You need someone to teach you the correct postures. Yoga is all about the correct form and proper breathing. Join a class first, then gauge if you need a personal trainer and then you can use DVDs too.

- **Outfit Misfit:** You will throw your legs into the air, twist your arms, squat and contort . . . Wear clothes that allow you to breathe and manage different positions.

- **Snack Stack:** Eat some fruit or a toast or upma 45 minutes before a workout. Working out on an empty stomach will make you feel weak and you will give up.

- **Session Aggression:** Don't do power yoga for more than 45 minutes or an hour. You might get exhausted and, honestly, your body doesn't need more than that.

- **Prime Time:** When the children are at school or the baby is napping, get it done with. I work out before 5 p.m. Later on, I'd rather spend time with the kids or unwind with my sister.

- **Doc Talk:** Consult your doctor before starting any exercise regimen. If you have a bad back, bad knees or other ailments, your yoga teacher can suggest asanas accordingly.

- **Space Race:** You don't need a large space to practise yoga at home. Just fit a clean, soft yoga mat near your bed and you're set. Make sure there are no pointy objects around that could hurt you while you twist and turn.

- **Travel Tips:** Once you master a few asanas and the surya namaskar, you can do them anywhere. Even when I travel with the children or for shoots, I always find time and space to do yoga.

- **Innate Meditate:** The final 10 minutes of a yoga session, spent in shavasana, calm your mind and centre you immensely. Don't consider it insignificant just because it does not help you lose weight! A tranquil mind helps you understand your body better and take the correct decisions, including what food to eat. When you're stressed, you eat anything that comes your way.

Remember that yoga is a practice of honouring yourself and your body. Rediscover your body and soul in a nurturing, self-supportive way. Find the time in your busy life to spend 10 minutes on yourself. The stresses of the day and world outside your yoga space might seem pressing and urgent but, ultimately, whether the dishes are put away and the laundry is done is not as important as whether or not you feel at home in your body and are in touch with the divinity within you. Start your yoga practice at home slowly, continue steadily and gently, and while you look at your hamstrings stretch, watch your spirits soar.

I saw dramatic results in my body and mind within a month of doing power yoga. I do it four times a week. Some people need to give themselves more time. Results from yoga can be seen if you do it diligently four times a week for three months at least.

For my power yoga, I need fast music to keep me pumped throughout my session. I play Rihanna, Adele, Pitbull, Jay-Z and other hip-hop artists. To meditate, I switch off all music, draw the curtains, and make the atmosphere tranquil. Having said that, it doesn't matter what music you listen to as long as you enjoy working out. A runner doesn't need wind in her hair; she just needs the road. You don't need external things to work out; all you need is determination.

Affirmation

I accept that my body is changing.

I trust my body.

I choose to be happy today.

Fitness after Pregnancy

'I'm a size 18!' I would shriek once the baby was out. 'I was a size 8!' I would whine. My doctor would just stand there and weigh me. I was hoping he would let me work out immediately so I could get back into my favourite jeans that I hadn't touched in months. 'Sorry Karisma, you've just had a caesarean! You need at least 40 days of absolute rest before you even start your walks. And no weights for the first 3 months. And don't even think about jogging,' she said, as she wrote out my diet and fitness charts.

I tried to reason with him: 'I'm an XL now—I used to be an S!' Enough said. Now he would understand.

But he just smiled and said, 'Soon you will be an S. But let there be no pressure on you from anyone. Even if the media hounds you, even if your family expects you to get back to normal, even if you're dying to get into those jeans, you have been through SURGERY! Be gentle with your body and I promise you that with this diet and fitness you will be back to your old self within 8 months to a year.'

And I was. I listened to my doctor.

Many women want to jump back into being skinny immediately after delivering a baby. It took you 9 months to put on that weight, so give yourself at least 9 months to lose it. That is the only way you can be healthy and keep it off. Otherwise, it will show on your face and you may balloon up again. I know this now after two babies and I'm so glad I did it over a period of 6–7 months. And I'll show you how.

For the first 2 months, you will feel very depressed that your weight is not falling off. It's a part of the post-partum depression which plagues many women. During pregnancy, you buy larger clothes as you put on weight and get bigger; after pregnancy, you wear the same clothes in descending order. The mistake a lot of mothers make is that as soon as they reach a medium size, they give up or they are okay wearing a large size and telling themselves, 'So what if I am wearing a large? After all, I've had a baby!' I would say don't give up till you fit into the clothes you used to wear before you got pregnant. Those last few kilos are always very difficult to shed but don't give up, because you will feel much better with those extra kilos off. It took me 3 months to lose those extra 3 kg. Just 3 kg. But I never gave up.

High Five: Five Tips before You Start Exercising

Tip 1

Get good help to look after your child while you're working out so your routine won't be interrupted. Else, make sure the child is well fed and fast asleep before you begin.

Tip 2

Don't overdo any exercise. Don't think you can do an hour a day and speed up the process. If you pull a muscle, you'll be back on bed rest for a long time, sister!

Tip 3

If you had a normal, uncomplicated delivery, you can start stretching exercises as early as the day after you give birth. But these should be very simple, non-stressful exercises, like leg stretches and Kegel exercises. If you've had a caesarean, it is best to wait until your stitches have healed.

Tip 4

If you hit the gym, consult a trainer. You might think you know the machines but you don't want any injury due to neglect.

Tip 5

You may want to pump out some milk and keep it aside to feed your child immediately after your workout, in case you're too tired to feed.

Throw Your Weight Around!

To lose weight gradually, you must aim to eat fewer calories than your daily calorie needs and also maintain or increase your exercise intensity. Do not go below 1200 calories per day unless you are on a medically supervised weight-loss programme or have consulted your doctor.

You need to do two things: calculate your BMR and your daily activity.

What is your BMR? Your BMR or basic metabolic rate is the rate at which your body is working while at rest. It is the minimum caloric requirement to sustain life if you were to lie in bed all day. This is determined by genetics, body surface area, age, weight and so on. A lower metabolic rate means it will take you that much longer to burn the calories you eat. Whatever you put into your mouth has calories and fat!

How do you calculate BMR?

Well, BMR = 655 + (9.6 x weight in kg) + (1.8 x height in cm) – (4.7 x age in years), where 1 inch = 2.54 cm and 1 kg = 2.2 lb. Here's an example: you are 30 years old, you are 5'6" tall (167.6 cm), and you weigh 120 lb (54.5 kg), which means that your BMR = 655 + 523 + 302 – 141 = 1339 calories per day.

What is your daily calorific need? It is the amount of calories you need to maintain your current weight. To lose weight, you need to eat 500 calories less than that every day. Your daily calorific need is calculated according to your age, whether you're breastfeeding, and how much exercise you're getting. Remember that breastfeeding also burns 350–500 calories per day for the first 6 months if there is no top feed for the child.

How do you calculate activity?

To incorporate activity into your daily caloric needs, do the following calculation:

- If you are sedentary: BMR x 20 per cent
- If you are lightly active: BMR x 30 per cent
- If you are moderately active (exercise most days a week): BMR x 40 per cent
- If you are very active (exercise intensely daily, for prolonged periods): BMR x 50 per cent
- If you are extra active (do hard labour or are in athletic training): BMR x 60 per cent

Add this number to your BMR. The result of this formula will be the number of calories you can eat every day and maintain your current weight. To lose weight, you'll need to take in fewer calories than this. As you lose weight, you can recalculate the formula to assess your new BMR.

I would seriously not recommend that anyone ever go below the 1200-calorie deficit. A drastic diet and intense exercise programme will only weaken you, and you will not have enough energy to play with or feed your child. It can also cause dark circles, stretch marks and terrible pigmentation. So do things gradually and remember that weight loss will happen if you stick to your regimen.

Women who have natural deliveries can recover faster and start exercising sooner. Women who have caesareans must wait much longer. Both my pregnancies were caesareans so I waited for 40 days before I started my walks. On the 41st day, I walked around my building for 10 minutes to see if my body could take it. After that, I took half-hour walks around the building first and then went to parks. I built up the speed and duration gradually. I didn't plunge into a brisk walk from day 1. The ideal time limit for a walk is 30–40 minutes. An hour is too long. I feel your stitches can open up if you overexert yourself and that will just put you back in bed. So, be cautious in the beginning. After 3–4 months you may consult your doc and start hard-core exercises.

The key is to exercise at least five to six times a week. I would take Sunday off to rest my body but I was very regular during the week. There is no excuse for not looking after yourself. After all, it is only 45 minutes a day. I do not believe that your body needs more that that anyway. In my experience, if your body has reached its capacity at 45 minutes, it has already shut down. So the extra 15 minutes will not help your body further.

Also, you cannot push your body beyond a certain point. After my second child, even though I wanted to work harder, my body started aching in places. I could not push myself on the treadmill as much as I wanted to. It depends on each person and each pregnancy and how much the body can take. You need to be gentle with yourself. Do not push your body so that you end up with a fracture or organ damage. Decide for yourself what and how much is right.

While working out, wear clothes that you can perspire in. Cotton is a good fabric. Wearing a salwar-kameez-dupatta hinders your walk, so wear a tracksuit ideally. Wear comfortable shoes with good soles to give your feet the padding they require.

Never Never Land: Five Workout Taboos

1. NEVER wear heels while working out. It can ruin your back and damage a nerve.

2. NEVER wear make-up. It hinders your skin from breathing. And you're going to sweat, which will smear your make-up. There is no point, really!

3. NEVER wear heavily embroidered clothes. You are not going for a fashion parade. You don't need to wear heavy zardozi clothes that are going to hamper your workout. You also don't need to wear your nice dresses or office wear to the gym. You'll only ruin them.

4. NEVER wear heavy perfume. A light deodorant will do. You don't need to smell like the Garden of Eden! Perfume mixed with perspiration can be overwhelming not only for you but also for the people working out in the gym with you.

5. NEVER wear heavy jewellery. Dangling earrings, big solitaires, large buckles and several bracelets are not only a health hazard but they can also get lost, stolen or caught in a machine. Keep your jewellery at home. Concentrate on your body.

During my first pregnancy, I was quite anxious about being so fat. I am a petite girl and I would think, 'Oh God! Will this ever go away?' It was not about being slim and trim and pretty—it was just about being myself! For all you mothers out there, I have to say, please take your time to figure out your own body. There is no need to race back into looking like a superstar. And please don't opt for surgeries to make you fitter. I have taken 24 kg off over a year and I've done it twice. Give yourself time.

As I already shared, I was very active throughout my second pregnancy. I was already a mother. I dropped and picked Samaira to and from school daily. I walked a lot every day, though not on a treadmill. Walking helps with your delivery as well. Since I was getting our Mumbai house done up, my mind was active. I think that is the best workout you can give yourself during your pregnancy—keep your mind active in the day and peaceful at night.

My Workout Regime

Day 41 Onwards till Month 3
Light walks, 5–6 days a week

Month 3 to Month 6
Pilates/cardio + weights, 6 days, alternating

Month 6 to Month 9
Boot camp (more on this in the chapter 'Boot Camp: Time to Kick Some Ass')

I had a personal trainer. There aren't many people who can afford one and that's perfectly fine. I needed someone else to push me a little harder. If you are determined, you can do it on your own or even have a relative call and check up on you to make sure you're pushing yourself every day.

My Routine from Month 3 to Month 6

Weeks 1–4
Alternate between cardio (40 minutes treadmill + 10 minutes elliptical/cycle) and gym (10 minutes walking warm-up + 50 minutes interval training)

Weeks 4–8
Alternate between cardio (45 minutes running in a park + slow stomach crunches) and gym (10 minutes warm-up + 60 minutes alternate between upper body and lower body)

Weeks 8–12
Alternate between cardio (freehand exercises like skipping, climbing stairs, running, walking briskly, all together) and gym (heavier weights)

After 6 months, I began to see results in my body. I needed to do something more then. I was getting tired of the gym and my body needed a change. Even though I had lost some weight and the inches had started coming off, I knew my mind was so bored that it was telling me to sit at home every time I wanted to work out. This wasn't good at all. It was then that I discovered Pilates, a form of stretching through machines that pulls your muscles so you feel you've had a hearty workout without all the grunting and sweating in a gym. You also need a trainer to show you what to do. I would thoroughly recommend Pilates to people who haven't tried it out. And there's yoga, of course—the most natural way to get that healthy and toned body.

Let me try and give answers to some questions you may have . . .

I'm so sleep-deprived! Can't I just go to bed while my kid sleeps? I'll lose weight later.

Absolutely. Get enough rest. When your kid wakes up, feed him, strap him to a stroller and take him out for a walk. Take along a maid who can look after him while you do a few laps on your own. This way, you've had your sleep and so has he. But you don't need to sit at home if you're not tired!

I have resumed work. Between spending time with child and meetings and presentations, I hardly have the time to work out.

Who says you can't work out with your child? Get a bouncing ball and bounce him on that while you do your stomach crunches. Run on the spot and see how that makes him laugh while you've burnt 100 calories. Do 10 minutes at a time to complete your whole hour every day. Take the stairs at work. Walk from the parking lot to the office. Pace up and down while thinking about your presentation slides. Every bit of exercise counts. On weekends, hit the gym. After all, you need some time for yourself too.

I live in a joint family. There is no space to work out at home. The gym is too far away.

Do 10 minutes of spot jogging and jumping jacks after the first 3 months. Walk around your building for 30 minutes, non-stop. And stop making excuses! Get an aerobics DVD and work out in your room. Lock it and tell them you're working out. Be firm.

I've had twins by caesarean. Will I ever be thin again?

Of course you will be. Take time to nurture your twins for the first 40 days and start walking slowly in the second month after delivery. There is no reason why you can't and shouldn't look like a movie star. Don't give up. Eat right to breastfeed right. And wear a stomach girdle for a year to suck in your stomach. You'll see the results soon enough.

I exercise 3 days a week. Is it enough to lose weight?

Sure. But you will take 2 years instead of 1! And after a year, you might just give up and carry all that weight around. If you have time for 3 days, make time for 5 days and push it to 6 days. The mind is a wonderful organ. You see, it makes us bored or lazy but can even make us motivated and strong. The body just complies. Use your head wisely! And if you can only do 3 days a week, then at least maintain that.

Top Tip

Okay, here's a secret I've never told anyone. It's the most important tip to lose weight.

Take a photo of yourself at the beginning of every month after delivery along with a record of your measurements and weight. Make that photo your phone wallpaper. Look at it when you go out to eat, look at it when you're tempted to bunk your workout, look at it . . . Looking at photos of your cute child won't motivate you; keep those in another folder. Before-and-after pictures of yourself will inspire you.

Affirmation

To see the change, I need to believe in myself.
I will take time out for my body every day.
I will not do anything drastic because I'm a
mom now and my baby depends on me.

Boot Camp: Time to Kick Some Ass

We're now hitting the last lap of our strict dieting and exercise regimen. It's the toughest phase because you've probably seen the results by now and you're almost ready to give up. JUST DO NOT!

It was 6 months after Samaira's birth, and I had shed 12 kg. It was momentous. I could have stopped and said, 'Hey, I look fine!' But I wanted to go the whole hog and prove that I could lose the entire 24 kg that I had gained. Bebo would tell me to start yoga but I didn't like the idea at all. I was a hard-core gym person. I'd tell her, 'Yoga doesn't make you sweat. How can you lose weight then? It will only tone your muscles but I need to lose weight first.' So I went back to my gym. Soon enough, I was bored. So 6 months after Kiaan, I tried yoga. Initially, it was tough. I would sweat and pant and try to figure out if it was really my thing. My yoga instructor came home every morning and, like clockwork, my body would wake up and be ready for the session. Soon enough, I saw not only the weight decreasing but also the inches melting away. Then I gave up everything else. I didn't need the cardio or gym routine. I started doing intense yoga every day and I was most satisfied with it.

I chanced on yoga late in my life but I don't want you to make the same mistake. I was a non-believer for long even though it was working so well for my sister. Yoga takes longer to show results but it's really good as it cleanses your body of toxins and helps you breathe better, sleep better. A mom goes through so many different emotions—dealing with the baby, managing the family, tossing about on sleepless nights—and yoga can be a great form of relaxation. With your doctor's advice, you can start it as soon as your 3 months are up.

To reiterate, after my first baby, I didn't do any yoga. I did the regular gym and cardio routines that helped me shake all the weight off. After my second baby, I did power yoga and that too shook the weight off. You can go either way but I would highly recommend that, if you can afford it, you should employ a personal yoga trainer. It helps you stay motivated and lose weight faster.

Do the Math: Calculate Your BMI

BMI is the acronym given to Body Mass Index, a statistic that is calculated from your weight and height and roughly correlates to the percentage of your total weight that comes from fat, as opposed to muscle or bone or organ. The higher a person's BMI, the higher the percentage of fat in his or her body. BMI is a tool used to approximate one's obesity potential. It does not account for variations in body type, such as big bones or broad frames or heavy musculature. It does work well for 'average' frames and bodies. To calculate your BMI, divide your weight in pounds by your height in inches squared, and multiply that by 703.

Formula: $(\text{weight}/\text{height}^2) \times 703$

So, if your weight is 150 lb (68 kg) and your height is 65" (5'5"), your BMI is $[150 \div (65 \times 65)] \times 703 = 24.96$. Phew! Now you can smile because that BMI places you in the normal weight range!

What does the BMI number indicate? Your BMI will place you in one of the following categories:

- Those with a BMI below 18.5 are considered underweight.
- Those with a BMI between 18.5 and 24.9 are considered to have normal weight.
- Those with a BMI between 25.0 and 29.9 are considered overweight.
- Those with a BMI of 30.0 and above are considered obese.

In addition to the BMI factor, those who have a waist size of more than 35 inches (for women) have a higher risk of obesity-related health problems such as diabetes, high blood pressure and heart disease. For me, BMI was just a benchmark to get back on track. While I knew I was in the slightly overweight category, it motivated me to get to the lower half of the normal category. I didn't want to be 24—I wanted to be 20, and the BMI helped me intensify my exercise a little more.

My Boot Camp Routine

Boot camp must begin when regular exercise fails. If you haven't seen a tangible change in your weight and figure after a few weeks, despite sticking to your exercise and diet regimens, you need to start on boot camp. Remember, you cannot start it from the very beginning; that will work against you because if your body gets used to such hard-core exercising, it may be difficult to maintain the pace later. If you don't have access to a gym or a personal trainer, do your boot camp at home but be regular. You can't do it for 3 days and give up. You have to go hard core for 6 days a week for at least a month, without fail.

With Weights: Session 1

You will need a pair of weights that you're comfortable with, say 4 kg dumb-bells, and a skipping rope. To warm up, stand straight and just move your head, 10 times from left to right and 10 times up and down. Jog on the spot 200 times. Touch your toes 20 times with your legs hip-width apart. Rotate your shoulders 20 times, 10 times in either direction. The main workout will be 100 skips, followed by a 30-second break, followed by 12 repetitions for 1 set of weight exercises. Do this on alternate days, using Sunday as a break for your body.

Chest/Bench Press

Lie on a ball, bench or floor with abs contracted. Begin with weights straight up over chest, elbows slightly bent. Bend elbows and lower arms until elbows are just below shoulder level. Contract chest and push arms up but don't allow weights to touch at the top.

Push-Ups

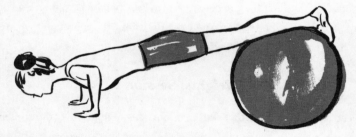

Begin in a push-up position on the floor, hands spread wider than shoulders. Rest your legs at the knees on the floor or on a ball for added intensity. Bend elbows and lower into a push-up, elbows at 90 degrees to the floor and abs in tight. Don't let your body sag in the middle. Push back to start and repeat.

Barbell Row

Holding a bar or weights in front of your thighs, bend knees and tilt torso forward to about 45 degrees, abs in tight. Take the weights out, following the line of the thighs, then squeeze the back to draw the weights in towards the belly button. Avoid this exercise if you have back problems.

Back Extension

Lie face down with hands either behind the back or lightly cradling the head. Lift upper body off the ground a few inches, keeping head and neck in alignment. For a challenge, lift feet off the ground keeping legs straight (knees don't have to be together), hold for 2–4 counts, lower and repeat.

Overhead Press

Sit or stand with weights in hands, elbows bent and weights next to shoulders. Straighten elbows and push weights overhead, palms facing each other and slightly in front of the head. Lower arms and repeat.

Front Raises

Stand with your feet hip-width apart, abs in, and torso upright, with medium weights resting in front of thighs. Lift arms to shoulder level, elbows slightly bent and palms facing the floor. Lower and repeat.

Concentration Curls

Kneel or sit in a chair and prop right arm on the inside of right leg, weight in hand and palm facing out. Contract the bicep to pull the weight towards the shoulder (without touching the shoulder). Lower and repeat.

Kickbacks

Bend torso forward until you're at 45 degrees or parallel to the floor, elbows bent next to ribcage. Contract triceps to straighten elbows, bringing weights up slightly above hips. Keep the abs tight and raise torso if this hurts your lower back or hamstrings.

Dips

Sit on a step or chair with hands next to thighs. Balance on your arms, moving your back to the front of the step/chair with legs straight (harder) or bent (easier). Bend elbows and lower body a few inches, keeping the shoulders down and the elbows parallel at 90 degrees. Push back up and repeat.

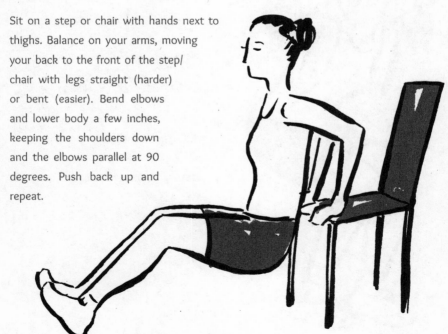

With Weights: Session 2

You must do your lower body workout three times a week, using Sunday as a break by getting a body massage! Do a set of jumping jacks 100 times, followed by a 30-second break, then lower-body repetitions of 12 for 1 set (40 minutes).

Weights Dead Lift

Stand with your feet hip-width apart. With shoulders back and back slightly arched, tip from the hips to lower the weight towards the floor (according to your flexibility) and slowly raise the back up, squeezing glutes, weight in the heels.

Squat with Barbell/Weights

Stand with feet spread wider than shoulders, barbell resting on the meaty part of the shoulders. Bend knees and, keeping chest up, lower into a squat. Keep abs in and knees behind toes. Push through the heels to raise back up and repeat.

Plié Squat

With barbell or dumb-bells, stand with feet wide apart, toes out. With knees in line with toes, lower into a squat. Knees should be behind toes. Push through heels and lift yourself back up.

Lunge

Using barbell or dumb-bells (or no weight) stand with feet apart, toes forward. Slowly lower into lunge position, keeping body erect and abs in, knees at 90 degrees to the floor. Push through the front heel, squeeze butt and slowly lift up to starting position (without locking knees). Repeat for one set and switch legs.

Straight Leg Glute Extensions

Using ankle weight (or no weight), balance on hands and knees, abs in and back flat. Straighten one leg and slowly lift yourself up, squeezing the glutes. Lower back down allowing toes to barely touch the floor. Repeat and then switch legs.

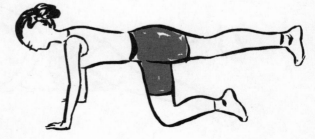

Straight Hip Extensions

Using ankle weight (or no weight) lie on the floor, abs in. Slowly lift one leg up until it is at 90 degrees to the floor. Lower back to starting position without relaxing.

Hamstring Rolls

Using exercise ball/chair, place heels or calves on ball and slowly lift butt up, tightening the abs. Roll ball towards butt, squeezing the hamstrings and keeping abs tight, back flat.

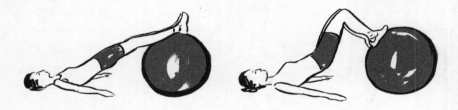

Hip Adduction

Lie on your side, one foot bent in front. Tighten abs and slowly lift the other leg as high as you can, keeping the leg straight, foot slightly flexed. Use ankle weights for added resistance.

Hip Abduction

Lie on your side, hips stacked, knees slightly bent. Lift top leg, squeezing the glutes, then lower back without completely relaxing. Use ankle weights for added resistance.

Depending on your body's stamina and flexibility, you should be able to move from skipping or jumping jacks to weights without a break for 30 minutes and then to 45–50 minutes. Gradually you should have about 1500 skips and 2 sets of weight sessions. You will feel exhausted by the end of a session. Give your body time to recover. Get a deep tissue massage to open up the muscles and let them heal.

Boot Camp Blunders

• Don't just work out extra repetitions on one body part, while neglecting the others. It doesn't become smaller that way. Your cardio routine will make it smaller and your weight training will tone it.

• Don't jeopardize your knees. Avoid locking your knees when you're lifting a weight, and don't allow your knees to shoot out past your toes in the squat, lunge, or leg press. If you feel knee pain during an exercise, stop immediately. Try another exercise and return to the one that gave you trouble after you've been training for a few weeks. Alternatively, perform a simpler version of the exercise, restricting the distance you move the weight.

• Don't perform more than 15 repetitions. Some people, afraid of developing bulky legs, use extremely light weights and perform 40 repetitions. You're not going to build up much strength this way, and you'll probably fall asleep in the middle of a set! You will also increase risk of injury from too much repetitive stress on your joints. If you feel that the weights are too light, use a higher weight set.

• Drink water! Hydrate yourself well during workouts. After the workout, have a nimbu-paani with a little rock salt and sugar.

• Give yourself 10 minutes to relax. After every workout, lie on the floor for 10 minutes, facing up and breathing normally. Take deep breaths to bring your heart back to normal. Don't start working on something else or immediately rush out the door or hop into the shower. Once your heartrate is normal, you can resume other activities.

Without Weights (Yoga)

Do not try yoga without a certified instructor. When I first started doing yoga, I was extremely stiff and couldn't even bend over to touch my toes. I was horrified. I had lost weight, I was in the correct BMI range, and I was feeling fit as a fiddle. I just needed to lose those few extra kilos that would take me from fit to fabulous! But when I started doing asanas, I realized my body was not as supple as I thought it was. Gradually, with a little bit of extra stretching every day, I was able to do a headstand without help. Yoga might take time to deliver results but it can transform your life. Today, I don't go to the gym or on walks. I only do yoga every morning. I can do it even on vacation in a hotel room and feel good for the rest of the day.

Spirited Away: Ten Benefits of Yoga

1. **Stress Relief:** Yoga can help reduce the effects of stress on your body. One of the benefits of yoga is that it aids relaxation and can lower the amount of cortisol in your body.

2. **Pain Relief:** Daily yoga can help ease the aches and pains of the body. Many people suffering from very serious diseases have reported less pain after daily yoga asanas or meditation.

3. **Better Breathing:** You will learn to take deeper, slower breaths with daily yoga practice. It will help improve your lung function and set off the body's relaxation response. This can be one of the most powerful benefits of yoga.

4. **More Flexibility:** You will notice your flexibility increasing, which will help with your range of motion. Yoga helps lengthen the muscles, tendons and ligaments in your body.

5.   **Increased Strength:** Yoga poses use all the muscles in your body and help you increase strength from head to toe. Daily yoga helps you strengthen your muscles close to the bones, which increases the support of your skeletal system as well.

6.   **Weight Management:** You will see the benefits of yoga on your weighing scale, yes! Yoga helps reduce the level of cortisol in your body. This helps your body burn fat and lose weight.

7.   **Improved Circulation:** Yoga will help improve your body's blood circulation. You will also see the benefits of yoga in the form of lowered blood pressure and pulse rates.

8.   **Cardiovascular Conditioning:** Even the gentlest style of yoga will help to lower your resting heartrate and increase your overall endurance. This is one of the important benefits of yoga, as it helps boost the amount of oxygen taken in during the daily exercises.

9.   **Focused Mind:** You can have greater coordination, memory skills, reaction times, and improved concentration skills by utilizing yoga for daily exercises.

10. **Inner Peace:** What more do you want? This is a primary reason that people do daily yoga. This is one of the most important benefits of yoga and is also one of the easier ones to attain.

The benefits of yoga are very far-reaching indeed. There is no other exercise avenue you can take recourse to that will address all of these issues in one simple session. For those of you who think yoga is too easy, I encourage you to try one class. You might find that it is just what you are looking for.

I must make a confession. I have been lucky enough to not get stretch marks after both my pregnancies. I think it was a combination of diet and the workout I did *before* I became pregnant, plus I had good genes. At least, I think so. But many women do get stretch marks.

What are stretch marks? They happen when the skin is stretched over a short period of time and it becomes thin and silvery and may appear scar-like. Doctors think some people get stretch marks because their bodies have higher levels of a hormone called corticosteroid. This hormone decreases the amount of collagen in the skin, which is sad because collagen is the protein that keeps our skin fibres stretchy. Here are a few ideas to prevent and reduce stretch marks.

Bar the Scar: Shoo Away the Stretch Marks

• Follow a good diet plan, with eight glasses of water a day, before and during pregnancy.

• Avoid the sun as much as you can. Never let your tummy get too dry. Moisturize with aloe vera during the day.

• Get yourself daily hot-oil massages as soon as your doctor allows it, after the delivery.

• Try rubbing in a mixture of two parts almond oil and one part cold-pressed wheatgerm oil; it has been used by women for generations.

• Make your own stretch-mark cream by mixing equal amounts of cocoa butter, olive oil, and vitamin E ointment. Apply twice a day, every day of your pregnancy.

• If a year after delivery, your weight is back to normal but the stretch marks persist, fear not and fret not. There are cosmetics, lasers and therapies to shoo them away.

I understand that there are many women who jump back into work as soon as they deliver because they don't have an option. There are also women who are surrounded by people, as they live in a joint family, and do not get any time from their duties to head to the gym or get a personal trainer. But seriously, you don't need any of that as long as you have determination!

Affirmation

I will not give up when I'm almost at the end.

My mom hasn't given me the genes to be fat.

I choose to be healthy. I choose to

maintain my ideal weight.

I will feel so much better when I succeed.

The Pursuit of Yummyness

Of Supersized Slacks and Home-Made Packs

What Goes Bump: Pregnancy Fashion

In 2005, when I was pregnant with my first baby, Samaira, the maternity wear range in India was very sad. There were no choices and everyone would just wear loose salwar-kameez! When my friends went abroad, I would ask them to pick up a dress or two that would make me look a little fashionable. I finally found a long black gown that wrapped tightly around my bump—I loved it! I wore it almost every time I went out. It was my father's birthday when I wore it for the first time . . . Honestly, I remember I just glowed with happiness.

But other than that, I'd never wear figure-hugging dresses to show off my baby bump. That just wasn't me. I've always been very traditional in my fashion sense. Some of my friends and I were pregnant at the same time and what divergent styles we had! One wanted to look hot and happening and took it to a totally different level. Another wore extra-loose clothes because she didn't want to harm the baby and also didn't want her bump to show, as she was paranoid about nazar. I think the key is to strike the right balance. It's nice to look a little fashionable and trendy, whatever you choose to wear. Dressing up makes you enjoy your pregnancy and you should be happy while you're pregnant.

My style was pretty different during both pregnancies. During Samaira's time, I wore more Indian clothes and dungarees. During Kiaan's time, I wore jeans, trackpants and cute dresses as I was moving around to get my house done, drop and pick up the school-going Samaira, finish chores and so on. I needed clothes that would neither make me uncomfortable in the Mumbai heat nor restrict my movement. I was also more brand aware by my second pregnancy. It had been 5 years since the last one and times had changed. Indian manufacturers had wised up to the demand of stylish maternity wear. There were specialized stores for mommies-to-be.

Guide to Gorgeousness: Fifteen Fashion Tips I Followed

1. Jean Transfer: Shift to maternity jeans! Invest in a couple of pairs that have a soft, elasticated waistband around the tummy—it's a huge help. I really enjoyed the snug feeling that my baby is taken care of and my stomach is supported. The jeans and tracks with T-shirts work best for pregnancy.

2. Dressing Down: At times, you may want to sit comfortably with your legs up or apart because of your bump, so slacks, cotton pants or maternity jeans would be a good option with a nice, loose shirt. When at home, at work or running errands, dress practically. Keep the fashionable dresses for parties.

3. Getting Shorty: Many women like wearing loose shorts so they can keep their legs free but I was always more of a pyjama girl. I wore loose trackpants with expandable soft elastic. I never liked showing off my legs to the help at home. But nowadays, most women are comfortable in shorts. What's more, their legs look great even during pregnancy! Short cotton dresses look very cute and casual. So if you feel like flaunting your legs, go ahead, get shorty!

4. Desi Duds: Patiala salwars are the best thing for the Indian weather. They are loose, they are soft and they cover your legs. Wearing them with a short cotton kurta and a bright dupatta can make you look rather cheery and stylish.

5. Side Orders: Always wear nice earrings, bangles, rings and so on. It makes you feel a little chic and glams up your outfits. Knot a scarf around your neck or wrap a colourful dupatta around your head. Bling it up! Be careful though that trailing accessories don't get caught anywhere.

6. Big Bag Theory: Carry a medium-sized slouch bag when you go out. It covers your belly from one side! I had a few large, colourful ones that I would choose from whenever I went out. Never stuff it, though, for that will make it heavy, make you uncomfortable and give you a shoulder problem. You just need a small bottle of water, a snack, your mobile phone, your wallet and some tissues in your bag as essentials.

7.   Fancy Dress: When I was carrying Kiaan, I had to attend a lot of weddings and here's what I realized—do not attempt a sari when you've got a baby bump because you won't know where to tie the knot, above or below the navel! Don't go for ghaghras either. Just wear an elegant salwar-kameez with minimal zardozi. Too much embellishment makes you feel hot and heavy and look like a Christmas tree!

8.   Big Foot: Wearing flats is a sensible option. Choose flats with a little bling if you're going for dressy, or you can get plain ones if you want to dress down. Also, buy shoes one size larger than your normal size because your feet will expand during pregnancy. I have small feet but they have grown, strangely! I was a size 35½ and I was wearing 36½–37 when I was pregnant but now my shoe size is 36! My doctor did tell me that my feet will grow and not return to their normal size and I asked him how that was possible . . . If your hips can go back to normal, how can your feet not?

9.   Heel Spiel: Think about the various kinds of occasions you will need footwear for and buy a few pairs in larger sizes. I bought one pair of everyday chappals, one pair of blingy chappals that I could wear when I went out and one pair of flat shoes, which would look nice with jeans and trousers. For evenings out, I had a pair with little kitten heels, which strangely enough I found painful, probably because I was so paranoid! But if you can, wear a little kitten heel to give you that elegant gait but no high heels please. They're really bad for your back. You get lovely designs in flats and chappals so why do you need 4-inch heels. For the rains, you must wear correct footwear like good-quality plastic slip-ons and rain boots. You can get colourful things and be fashionable but be careful about quality, so you don't get any diseases from the rainwater muck.

10. Overall Oomph: When I was carrying Kiaan, I had two pairs of denim dungarees. Loose and roomy, they got clipped on by buttons near my chest and covered most of my body. And they looked hip. I loved them. 'Boyfriend' jeans also look very cool with a snug-fitting T-shirt.

11. Basic Black: I am a very pro-black person. In fact, I either wear black or white so one of my chappals was black, the other was white and my evening shoes were black! Of course, they matched my clothes, which were also either black or white. Many of my friends, however, wore several colours during their pregnancy and loved it and looked amazing. Perhaps, I should have worn some more colour too . . .

12. Seasonal Style: Because we celebrated Christmas in Delhi and Pataudi when I was carrying Kiaan, I needed warm coats. I had two very beautiful coats; I still have them. Winter dressing is fun when you're pregnant because it looks so cute. You know what I enjoyed most while pregnant? That my body temperature rose! Usually, I freeze all the time, all year, but here I was feeling just perfect, even in winter.

13. Viva Velour: I bought three Juicy Couture tracksuits made of velour. I wore them at home and even while going out for chores. Often, you don't want to change every time you go out of the house and these comfy designer tracksuits in bright colours and made of ultra-soft velvet are just right for that.

14. No Lycra: I detest Lycra. I think it's the worst material to ever have been invented. My friends swear by it though. They loved wearing Lycra bandage dresses and felt that a little cotton mixed with Lycra clothing hung better than regular cotton clothes. I always stuck to cotton in the summer and wool in the winter.

15. Upper Case: I had short-sleeved T-shirts and a few spaghettis in different colours. But soon I saw that my normally thin arms were getting flabby. I had to cover them up, but how? I hated wearing full-sleeved shirts! So when I had to go out, I'd simply don a cardigan over my spaghetti!

What I'd like to emphasize is that you don't need to overspend to get stylish pregnancy clothes. Do make sure the quality of the clothes is high and they will last you a few months. You will ideally use these clothes from the fifth month through to the ninth, and may even wear them for the first 5 months after the baby, till your diet and exercise help reduce your size. That's 8–9 months of wearing the same outfits, so get good quality and a good assortment.

You don't need to invest in too many clothes either. You may look amazing in a particular shirt but you don't' need to buy it in all the available colours! Maternity fashion is all about mixing and matching, layering and accessorizing. If you're a working woman, no one is going to expect you to come dressed in Prada every day. You need to wear things that are comfortable for your pregnancy and for your lifestyle. Copying your friends' choices may not work for you.

Haute Howlers: Five Pregnancy-Fashion Blunders

1. **Inner Error:** Support is important! Incorrect underwear is disastrous. Thinking that you can squeeze your ever-growing breasts into the same old, pre-preggers bra will do more harm than good. Invest in good bras that have enough cup support and do not ride up at the back. You don't need more than the basics—a beige, a black, a white—as you will need to keep buying as your size increases. I eventually had nine maternity bras because my size went up so much. None of them were underwired though; underwiring cuts into your skin while you sleep. And as your stomach grows, it is painful. You should also buy colourful panties that make you feel nice. I never wore thongs or lace underwear. They would be itchy and very uncomfortable.

2. **Material Girl:** It is important to pay attention to the fabric you're going to wear next to your skin. Cotton is always best for your skin. It absorbs sweat and lets your skin breathe. Undergarments and clothes in good-quality cotton are the best, I feel. Avoid Lycra, zardozi, silk, chiffon, etc.—these can be worn occasionally when you want to go out or need a change.

3. **Shape Shifters:** Cute baby-doll dresses, empire-line kurtas and V-neck outfits are the best cuts for maternity clothes. They pull attention to your ample bosom and make you look like a yummy mummy. Avoid cuts that make you feel self-conscious.

4. **Purani Jeans:** Do not squeeze into your old clothing. If you've outgrown a shirt, let it go even if it is your favourite colour! If the zipper is not going further, buy larger pants. Don't try and get into a smaller size because only a month is left and you feel there's no point in buying something for just a month. Hey, you still need to be comfortable for that one month!

5. **OMG OD:** Overdoing it is plain silly. Everyone can see you're pregnant. You can't hide it. So don't divert attention by looking like a clown. Wearing excessive colour, make-up or jewellery will make you look ridiculous. Choose what you want for the day and develop your own fashion sense.

Fashion changes. It has changed from my mom's time. She used to wear a dupatta to cover the bump or wear loose clothes so that the bump would not be too visible. Like I said, you don't have to flaunt it everywhere but it's a beautiful thing so there's no harm in showing it off a bit if you're looking nice.

If you're going to stick to ethnic wear, a chiffon dupatta looks rather pretty. I am not a big stole person. If I'm going traditional, I will go totally traditional. But stoles look nice on some people who can wrap them around with jeans and a nice shirt or kurti. Whether you're going to go ethnic or chic, you must feel good about yourself. Fashion is not something you ape from others. It's a trial-and-error thing; go for colours and cuts that suit your body. Be fashionable. Be trendy. Be happy with your body.

After the babies were born, I think I spent all my days in kaftans! Since I was at home, I got a tailor to stitch kaftans with zippers or buttons down the front to allow me to breastfeed. A whole new wardrobe had to be made for just this period. I'm glad that I had thought of this earlier and got these soft paisley kaftans and shirts made, as well as picked up a few other things, beforehand. You don't have time to pick out clothes once you deliver. It's best to pick one outfit and tell the store to keep the rest on hold for you. When people come over and you don't want to be seen in a kaftan, you can slip on a nice shirt with zippers or buttons in front and tights or skinny jeans that are stretchable around your stomach and thighs.

Outfits for After: Five Postnatal Essentials

1. **Feeding Bras:** You will need three to four good-quality feeding bras since you will probably be feeding for a few months. Make sure they are very comfortable.

2. **Feeding Pads:** Since your breasts will inevitably leak, you will need feeding pads to soak the extra milk. It's a natural thing but you don't want to walk around with big, wet patches on your shirt! At night, you want to sleep comfortably. So use feeding pads and change them frequently.

3. **Shirts and Kaftans:** Front-open shirts and kaftans will make life much easier since you won't be struggling to lift your shirt and exposing your midriff every time you feed your child. Get darker colours so even if your breasts leak, it won't show.

Shirts in stretchable fabrics, which you can pull up and down easily, would work if you don't like the button concept.

4.   Stoles and Dupattas: Wherever you're going, you can take your child and feed her. All you need is a stole that covers your child's head and your breast while you do so. You may not be able to pump enough milk to carry in a bottle and your child may still be hungry. You can easily feed her if you cover yourself and avoid feeling indecent in public.

5.   Velcro Band: This awesome stretchable Velcro band that holds your stomach snug is the best thing invented for mothers. Within 48 hours of the children being born, I put on the Velcro band. It held my tummy in place and I often felt that it sucked my stomach in. It does give a lot of support to the stomach and brings it back into shape quicker.

After your baby is born, you will want to have a toned body quickly but it is just not possible. It will take time and dedication. Meanwhile, you can camouflage it! You don't have to look like a size 0—you can look voluptuous and quite the yummy mummy if you just follow a few fashion trends.

Va Va Vogue: Five Post-Delivery Fashion Tricks

1.   Empress's New Clothes: Start wearing empire-line dresses with V-shaped necklines. If you find an empire-line shirt or kurti, you can wear it with tights or slacks or even skinny jeans.

2.   Hue Dunnit: Darker colours hide fat better. So if you're going to get an outfit, remember to pick out dark fuchsia, dark blue, olive green and so on, instead of whites and pastels.

3.   Foot Notes: Now that the baby is out, you have your centre of gravity all to yourself. But you still don't want to trip and fall in high heels. This is the time to get one or two block-heel shoes that give you height and make your legs look slimmer.

4.   Drape Escape: If it's winter, you can wear jackets, coats and shawls that drape your body to camouflage the pregnancy weight. If you've delivered in the summer, wear baby-doll dresses with stoles in different colours, a shirt with a waistcoat, and high-waisted skirts that end at your knees.

5. Ban That Bling: Heavy-duty embroidery or embellishments like zardozi just make you look fatter. Delicate lace at the neck or at the bottom of the outfit or a few borders stitched on to the outfit can give it a distinct class.

The smartest thing to do is get a good tailor. You can transform your maternity wear into regular wear if the tailor can alter your clothes slightly. Shirts with sleeves can become cap-sleeved ones. A cardigan can be stitched on to a dress you're bored of to make it a full-sleeved dress! You can change hemlines and neck silhouettes, or just buy new fabric to make something cool that you saw in a catalogue. If your slacks or jackets feel large, get them altered as and when you lose weight. You can visit discount stores and street bazaars to pick up trendy things that are affordable. You don't need to spend a bomb on something and then feel bad that it's maternity wear.

You must also realize that you need to give your body time to get back into your regular clothes. Just because you've had a baby doesn't mean you can't still wear maternity clothes. But don't make it a habit—you cannot camouflage forever! I set myself a deadline. Three months after the babies came, I gave away all my maternity clothes. I made it a point not to be comfortable any more. I wanted

to get back into my old jeans and I felt more committed to losing weight once I knew there were no stretchy fabrics to cover my fat. When I'd gone to the hospital, I'd carried a tight dress for the return journey. I realized soon that a high expectation from myself was not going to get me into that dress. So I advise you to carry a loose dress but also to throw it away after 5 months. You don't want to be the same weight as when you walked out of the delivery room even after 5 months. You want to be the one getting into the tight dress!

Affirmation

I won't be frumpy—I'll be fabulous!

I won't stop focusing on myself.

I will take time out to fix myself for myself!

Glow and Afterglow: Beauty Tips for Pregnancy

My grandmother used to oil my hair every day. I remember how Bebo and I used to sit in front of her and she used to say that oiling our hair would make it long and lustrous and I can't remember anyone having better hair than her. So when I got pregnant, I decided to not go in for any beauty therapies for my hair but just oil it every week and follow up with a thorough hair wash. I trimmed my hair every 6 weeks since it was growing at a rapid pace and the trim made me look neat and tidy. I was very particular about avoiding any treatments with chemicals. I banned hair colouring, I even banned hair spas. I applied natural products to my hair whenever I remembered to, and I never went overboard. Even after I delivered, when my hair was falling out in tremendous clumps, I didn't panic. I knew that it is a natural tendency and I kept oiling my hair every week to give it the strength it needed.

The one thing that helped me before and after pregnancy was having almonds. I'd soak eight to ten almonds overnight and gobble them up every morning, after peeling them. I didn't miss a single day for 9 months and through the 4 months after delivery. It kept my skin glowing, my hair healthy and any acidity in check. I also had two walnuts every day. I'm a firm believer in everything natural from food to treatments, and from diets to fitness solutions.

You must also moisturize your body and face every day because pregnancy tends to dry up your skin. Use a moisturizer with an aloe vera or cocoa butter base to keep your skin supple and soft and, most important, to prevent stretch marks. Take care to find a good face moisturizer that doesn't give you a rash.

Pregnant and Pretty: Ten Beauty Tips

1. **Safe Make-Up:** Please don't experiment with new products at this time. If you've been using something and it has worked for you, stick with it. Using new make-up can give you a rash or have some other horrible effect that will have you rushing to the doctor!

2. **Simple Make-Up:** At times, a light kajal and a touch of lip gloss is all you need to look pretty. Heavy foundation and tonnes of make-up can react with your skin and also make you look extremely pretentious. You are glowing with pregnancy hormones—maximize it!

3. **Safe Hairstyle:** Don't get a radical haircut at this stage. A good haircut can do wonders but don't experiment with chopping off those tresses or getting extensions. You might just hate it and be in a bad mood till it grows out, and that could be till after the baby is born! Instead of going all out, get a trim every 6–8 weeks to keep your hair neat and tidy.

4. **No Chemicals:** Colouring, bonding, curling, extensions and hair spas are all chemical treatments for your hair. All those chemicals go into your scalp, and that is

dangerous even though you might be thinking right now that the scalp and the tummy are too far apart for them to affect the baby. Believe me, they do! If you hate your hair so much, get a nice cap when you go out but avoid chemical products.

5. **Lots of Water:** Hydrate yourself. You're drinking for two. You need to up your water intake. This also helps you reduce acne and any other skin blemishes.

6. **No Body Art:** You should not get any piercings or tattoos done while you're pregnant. The ink can be harmful for your skin, and the sharp pain can cause a sudden contraction that could escalate into a medical emergency. If you already have a tattoo on your belly or lower back, consult your doctor about the precautions you need to take for it.

7. **No Facials or Peels:** You may see discoloration, acne and dark circles on your face while you're expecting. These are hormonal changes that will go away. Be patient. Getting a facial or a chemical peel might just make it worse by activating glands that may spread the condition. Wait till you've delivered. In fact, if you stick to your light exercise, healthy diet and adequate rest, you may not even develop these problems.

8. **Manicures and Pedicures:** It's nice to be pampered while you're expecting. You can get yourself manicures and pedicures, and get your nails painted in pretty colours to feel nice. Get your legs and hands massaged but instruct the masseur to stay away from your ankles. They have certain pressure points that may induce contractions and you totally want to avoid that!

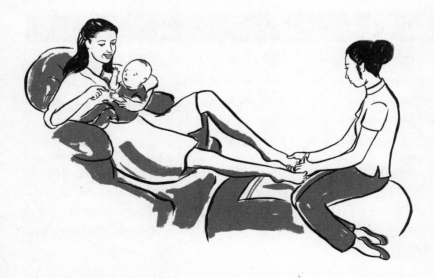

9. Control Puffy Eyes: Steep two camomile teabags in hot water. Take them out and let them cool. Apply one bag to each eye and let it stay for 5 minutes. It's really soothing, even if you don't have puffy eyes.

10. Prevent Stretch Marks: If you can, use pure cocoa butter and aloe vera to moisturize your body. It helps prevent and reduce stretch marks. What's more, it makes you smell divine!

Yummy Mummy: Five Postnatal Tips

1. Ghee Gaga: Your breasts might crack and you may feel extreme discomfort while you're feeding. Keep your breasts dry. Wipe off any extra milk after the baby has fed, then apply desi ghee to your nipples and wear your bra. You can apply it as often as you like, as it's a natural remedy and won't affect the baby either. It's far better than any chemical nipple cream!

2. Sun Safe: You must always, always wear sunscreen before, during and after pregnancy to shield your skin from UV rays. Just 15 minutes before you step out of the house, apply a little bit to your face and hands and any body part that will be exposed to the sun. Buy one with an SPF of 30–40. In any case, avoid being in the sun for long periods.

3. Scrub Dub: Keep your skin clean by regular exfoliation. Instead of using regular soap, use a scrub once a week on your face and body to remove dead skin cells and boost blood circulation.

4. Shower Power: Pregnancy and feeding make you hot and sweaty. Your body temperature rises. To keep cool, take regular showers with a mild soap or bath gel. It will keep you feeling fresh and light. Remember to wear fresh underclothes after your shower as well!

5. Pack Perfect: You can apply home-made face packs to keep your skin cool or give you an extra glow. Make sure you apply these after your child has gone to sleep so you don't scare him away! Here are some packs that you can easily rustle up at home.

Home-Made Face Packs for Moms

For Dry Skin: Simply Avocado
For a basic moisturizer, mash half a ripe avocado and apply it to your face. Leave on for 15–20 minutes. Rinse off.

For Dry Skin: Avocado and Honey
For a little luxury, mash half an avocado and mix with ¼ cup of honey. Apply it to your face and leave on for 15 minutes. Rinse off. It's a great moisturizer.

For Oily Skin: Grapefruit and Sour Cream
A great skin refresher, this mask is perfect if your skin feels oily and tired. Beat an egg white till it's fluffy, add 1 tsp of sour cream and 1 tsp of grapefruit juice and mix well. Apply to your face for 15 minutes, and rinse off with warm water.

For Oily Skin: Strawberries
If you can live with putting strawberries on your face instead of in your mouth, this is a wonderful recipe for oily skin. Mash and mix ½ tsp of lemon juice, an egg white, 1½ tsp of honey and ½ cup of strawberries. Apply to your face and leave on for at least 10 minutes. Rinse off with warm water.

For Oily Skin: Oatmeal and Almond

This mask makes your skin feel very smooth. I've used it for many years and like it a lot. It looks awful when applied to your face, however, so don't scare your children or neighbours! Cook 2 tbsp of instant oatmeal porridge. Don't add salt. Grind 1 tbsp of almonds to a fine meal. Mix with the porridge. Apply when cool enough and leave on for 10–15 minutes. Rinse off.

For Exfoliation: Sugar

This is a really great face scrub. Mix a cup of brown sugar with 1–3 tbsp of milk and apply to your face leave on for 15 minutes. Then scrub it off with a wet washcloth. Simple and effective!

For Exfoliation: Oatmeal Scrub

Grind 2 tbsp of oatmeal and mix with enough yogurt to make a thick paste with good consistency. Apply to your face and massage it in gently. Leave on your face for 10 minutes, then rinse off.

For the Eyes: Cucumber

Grate and strain ½ cucumber and refrigerate the juice. Add a little rose water to the cold cucumber juice. Dip two pads of cotton wool in this mix and place on your eyes for 5 minutes. Feel the stress melt away!

For the Eyes: Black Tea

Prepare black tea and allow it to cool. Soak cotton balls in cold tea and use as eye pads. Tee off!

Just like my sense of style, my beauty techniques too have evolved over the last 20 years. When I first got into the film industry, I was such a novice. I did what the director told me to do and went along with whatever the make-up artist said suited me. It was a very slow learning process for me. In fact, it was very different back when I joined, for everyone—we had no idea what beauty products to use, what styling to adopt and so on. But we learnt and eventually got the hang of it all.

I finally understood that I needed to go from being a young teenager to a young woman and how I put on my make-up had a lot to do with it. Make-up products have also become varied and extensive. I still use things that are natural and suit me. And it's a compliment that many people still admire my style.

Vision 2020: My 20-Minute Beauty Routine

5 minutes: Take a shower. It's important to feel fresh and clean.

2 minutes: Moisturize your skin—I do this daily.

3 minutes: Clean your face with a face wash, pat it dry and sit in an air-conditioned room till your face cools down. If you put on make-up in a humid room, it will cake and crack!

5 minutes: Apply a light foundation to your face if you're going out to a fancy place, else let your skin glow naturally. I don't use powder but a good powder in the same colour as your foundation evens out your skin tone. Don't use a lighter foundation just to look fairer; it makes you look like a ghost! Find a foundation that matches your skin tone.

3 minutes: Spend some time putting on eyeliner or kajal. I just use kajal and I'm all set. If you want smoky eyes, use good products and clean brushes. Try mascara to brighten your eyes.

1 minute: Blush or bronzer. Never both.

1 minute: Lip liner—lipstick—gloss. Never use just a lip liner since it's very dark. You can, however, just use a lipstick, put a tissue paper on top to blot it, put some powder around the lips, and then reapply lipstick with some gloss. The lipstick stays on longer.

You can always get a nice blow-dry in the day if you know that you're going out later in the evening. I have someone who comes home and blow-dries my hair in about 30 minutes; else, I go to a salon for a quick styling. Let me tell you, I even get my waxing done at home. India is so convenient for these things. I get my manicures and pedicures at home because I want to be around the kids instead of going off to the parlour for hours. Over the years, I've learnt how to do my own make-up. So now, I don't have a make-up artist or hairstylist or fashion stylist for any occasion; I put together my look on my own. I like the simple and elegant look, and I stick to that. A few fashionable accessories here and there complement my look.

I don't usually go along with beauty trends though I must tell you that I recently tried the tangerine lipstick fad. Till then, the only thing I'd experimented with was putting a steel-grey eyeliner instead of a black one and there I was trying out orange lip colour . . . Obviously, Bebo has some effect on me!

Chic Trick: Five Fashion Trends I Follow

1. **Shine On:** I use a touch of bronzer on my face and other body parts to lend a bit of shimmer. Don't put on too much though, for you'll end up looking ridiculously shiny!

2. **Two Hoots:** I stick to two accessories ONLY: necklace and ring, or earrings and ring, or earrings and bangles. Pick two that you want to highlight and wear only those two.

3. **Arm Candy:** A nice handbag like a snazzy clutch can also be an accessory, especially when going out in the evening. When you've dressed to kill, a dowdy bag will only kill the look!

4. **Skin Sin:** A hint of shoulder, a bit of cleavage, nice long legs or a sexy back—pick one that you want to highlight. If you do them all, you'll look like a tramp and be labelled one as well! Be classy with your skin show. Highlight the area you're most comfortable with on that day.

5. **Colour Code:** I'm a pretty black-and-white girl. I haven't experimented too much with colour. However, I have a few things in a single colour that looks absolutely fabulous on me. Many women know how to match colours well. A friend once wore an animal print shirt with skinny yellow jeans and gold accessories. She looked amazing! Try out combinations that you're comfortable with and that look good on you. Go splash on some magenta or turquoise blue right now!

I know how a lot of mommies feel the pressure to look good right away. Well, it's not going to happen. I enjoyed the process of losing weight, getting fit, finding my fashion sense, figuring out my beauty products and finally reaching a state of bliss. It will take each one her own process. Don't rush it. You need to have a lot of self-confidence. Don't let anyone get you down about how you look. You've just had a baby. Your skin is changing according to the hormones in any case. Give it time to settle instead of smothering your face with products to look good.

Affirmation

Each day is different.

I can only grow from here.

I will experiment till I get it right.

I will be confident of who I am,

irrespective of how people see me.

The Motherhood of Travelling Pants

Of Office Bags and Luggage Tags

Briefcase Mommy: Balancing Work and Motherhood

The first time I left Samaira home and went to work was the most horrible day of my life. I felt as if I was the worst mother in the world for abandoning my child. I could hardly concentrate on work and kept calling intermittently to find out if she was okay. When I finally reached home, I saw that Samaira was happily playing with my mother and the nurse who had been looking after her the whole day. She hadn't missed me at all! Of course, she was 5 years old when I finally stepped out to do something but many women will not have the option of staying at home for as long as I did.

I didn't go back to work because I had to. I went back to work because I wanted to. And yet, the angst of separation is as strong whether the child is a few months old or a few years old.

I remember the time I had to travel for a shoot when Kiaan was a year old and I had started working. I was at an airport and heard a baby crying and looked around frantically to see if it was my child! I felt in my heart that my child was crying out for me, back home.

I would be in tears every time I left home because I felt guilty about leaving my kids behind. Gradually, it became better. It always gets better.

Also, I had many people berating me to 'get a life' and there was no harm if I chose to step out for work or other life commitments. I hadn't gone out for so long—it was high time I went out for myself. Many women give up their jobs because they have separation anxieties. I firmly believe that you must learn from me. I spent several years looking after my children and hesitating to step out, thinking that they would not grow up to be great human beings if I left them alone! I was being paranoid. If your work makes you happy, please go and work—because a happy mother will radiate that happiness on to her children. Never lose your identity because it is your identity that helps you mould your children as well. They have far more respect for a woman who is good at her job and manages a house than someone who can only do one thing and is bitter about it. So never ever lose yourself.

Motherhood isn't easy—whether it's your first child, your second or your third. You need to give enough time to the baby, his siblings, his father, and also everything else in your life. If you're a career woman, you need to stay abreast of everything that's happening in your field. If you're home for a year or two, you need to keep in touch with your colleagues at work or just keep tabs on the business, surf the internet to stay updated, learn a new skill from home perhaps or be tuned into your company's policies and impulses so that when you join back after a sabbatical, you won't feel all at sea but be in charge and in sync. A friend of mine took 6 months off after her child was born and used that time to learn how to use Microsoft Excel and make PowerPoint presentations; so when she joined work, she was able to wow them with some new skills.

The glamour industry is tougher on women. We need to be in shape before we get back to work. I had the choice of not having to work, and I opted for it. Some TV actors give it a shot—they go into labour one week and come back to work a week later. I really don't know how they do it but it's incredible to be so focused.

Also, with TV, the character needs to be seen continuously for the audience to relate to the show. In the case of films, you can choose to not do a film for a year and just complete the ones you have signed up for.

If, however, you choose to be a stay-at-home mom like I was and give up your career, do not feel the pressure from your family members to get back to work. You have taken time to make this beautiful child and if you feel you need to spend more time bonding with your baby, then take that time and don't bother about the world. Find the balance and the peace to make a decision and be happy with it.

Mama Dilemma: To Work or to Stay at Home?

Here are some of the factors you must consider in taking this tough decision.

- **Moolah Mantra:** The most important factor is your financial status. The pregnancy and the delivery might have cost you quite a bit and acquiring maternity clothes, baby products and hiring a nanny might also have depleted your finances a bit. If you feel you can take time off and still have sufficient funds to manage for some time, be a stay-at-home mom. If you have family that can support you as well with money, you have a choice again. But if you want to make the extra bit of money and live a little better, it's always practical to hire a nanny who can do the basics like bathe, feed, clean, and sing the child to sleep while you are away—you can spend time bonding with your baby later, for a few hours every day.

• **Heart Smart:** Let your feelings dictate your life, for once. Don't be bullied by your in-laws into going back to work at the earliest. On the other hand, if you feel you can be a good mother only by being a working mother, then don't feel guilty about going out either. Millions of children with working parents have grown into successful, loving adults. The same goes for children with a parent staying at home with them. When people comment on how you just sit at home every day, simply ignore them. You're far stronger for looking after your child than someone who has to just meet deadlines.

• **Doc Speak:** If you've had a C-section, your doctor will tell you when you are fit enough to go back to work. Also, if you've had any tear or surgery while delivering, you need to be careful that you heal completely before you get back to work. Any form of infection could put a strain on your body and subsequently harm your child.

• **Time Frame:** Most women feel that the child might get closer to the caregiver/nanny if they themselves are not around. This won't happen if you make it a point to spend quality time with your child at the beginning and end of the day. You can always dedicate a few minutes early in the morning before you head off to work and then a couple of hours once you come back. This is vital if you want to bond with your child. You need to make their timings your priority. If you leave before they awaken and return after they sleep, you'll miss out on their growth. Strike a smart balance between work timings and kid timings.

• **Home Work:** If you can manage working from home while the baby sleeps or if you can prioritize time for yourself and have a job that doesn't need you in office every day, it will be perfect. But working from home is tough since you do compromise on dedicating the required time to the job. While you can work for 10 straight hours in office, working from home might only allow you 3—4 productive hours in a day. Flexitime is great but it does mean that you might not get that promotion very soon!

I had already been working for 15 years by the time I had my first child. I was ready to be a full-time mother. But even after I got pregnant, I was finishing a film, my TV show and shooting an ad film, right up till my eighth month. So when I finally delivered Samaira, I was ready to put up my feet and be a stay-at-home mom. I wanted to take a break, enjoy motherhood and cherish my newborn. When I was carrying Kiaan, I was working throughout my pregnancy, till the very end. After his birth, I went back to work wthin 6 months. I thoroughly enjoyed pampering him as well. I didn't need to wait longer than that to get back to work. I felt it was the right time for me then. Every woman has to find her own comfort level. And if you can balance work and motherhood, then kudos to you.

Now when I go back to work, Samaira asks me if I'm going for an ad shoot or a film shoot. When she sees me on TV in an ad, her friends discuss it with her and she feels very proud. I feel very humbled that I've done something that makes her happy and makes her realize that I'm more than just a mom to her. I already have a considerable body of work behind me but I want to keep striving for my children to be happy and proud of me and I think I have a long way to go for that.

The thing is that I could go back to work after the babies because I had tremendous help from early on. Without the right infrastructure and support at home, it becomes difficult to get back to work, especially here in India. Abroad, there are many crèches and reliable babysitters for working parents to leave their kids with. Here, we don't have those options. But we do have maids, ayahs, nannies and extended families. I made full use of that network. You should too!

Negotiating Nanny: How to Manage Your Maids

- **Be Gentle, Be Appreciative:** Maids in India have egos. Big egos. They do not like being spoken to curtly and they do not like to be abruptly instructed by a woman they do not know. They come with the feeling that they already know everything. So while training them to do things your way, speak gently and when they do it right, appreciate it. Always say 'please' and 'thank you'!

- **Fix Routines, Set Menus:** If your daily routine is fixed and there are more or less set times for things like meals and baths and walks, the staff always knows what to do when, instead of idling around the kitchen, having tea and gossiping. You must let them know that the timetable has to be followed strictly, unless there's been a deviation with the baby sleeping longer or feeling unwell. And if there has been something unusual, they must always inform you. Also, set the child's menu for the whole week or else the cook or nanny will make anything and give it to the hungry child. A little compromise can be allowed once in a while but not on a regular basis.

• **Set Boundaries, Make Rules:** Let the help know where they can go, what they can use, who will be in charge if there is a crisis and they can't get through to you—all this helps create better communication channels. Always be respectful of what the maid has done in the day and spend some time with her asking her what she did with the child and if she had any problems that you can manage for her. In my house, I do not allow the children to watch TV if I'm not around. It's easy for the help to put on the TV so the kids can sit glued to it the whole day while they are on their cell phones! If you set the rules, people will follow them.

• **Demand Hygiene:** You must make sure that the maid is clean and hygienic at all times. If she is a 12-hour maid, make sure she has had a bath in the morning. Make sure she washes her hands regularly and uses a hand sanitizer before picking up the newborn baby. She also needs to wash her hands after she uses the toilet. Teach her to cover her nose with a clean tissue every time she sneezes. Not only is her cleanliness important, how she cleans the baby is important as well. Teach her to sterilize feeding bottles and nipples, change your child's diaper, change his clothes if he has puked, and so on.

• **Share Info:** It's always good to keep a list of important numbers in an easily accessible place, say on the refrigerator. These would include your mobile number, your husband's number, your family doctor's number, your local hospital's number and so on. You can also keep the child's medical history near the telephone, listing blood group and any allergies. If your maid doesn't know how to read, feed the numbers into her cell phone or into your landline on speed dial so she can hold down just one number and you may be reached in case of any emergency.

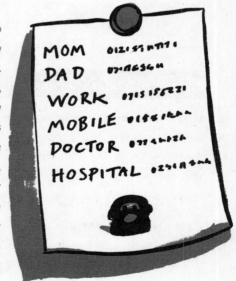

- **Delegate Duties:** In case you get a governess who has been trained as a caregiver or if your maid is literate, give her additional duties like reading to the child for a few minutes before he sleeps. A story time can be established and she can also help with homework in case you cannot.

- **Limit Chores:** Unless specified when you're employing her and negotiating her salary, do not give her any additional household chores like laundry, dusting, mopping, etc. If she has been hired only to look after your child, giving her extra work may make her feel short-changed. If you see that she needs more work, ask her if she would like to earn more by doing specified chores. Otherwise, don't push your luck—she will leave and you will be stuck!

- **Offer Comfort:** If you have a live-in maid, purchase some of her personal items as perks. Give her two sets of clean sheets and towels to use separately from the rest of the household and instruct her to wash these every week. Give her a comfortable place to sleep in. A good mattress and a working fan are essential for any person. Also, buy her toiletries on a regular basis or give her a separate amount of cash for what she wants to buy. A little extra care for someone who cares for your child goes a long way.

- **Invent Language:** If you have a maid who doesn't understand your language but is good with the child, start by creating your own body language. Show her how to communicate things and try to learn a few words in her mother tongue so you can communicate with her. Ask her to bring someone who can translate a few things for you and her. Slowly, find a groove with her.

- **Clarify Holidays:** Right up front, tell your maid how many days in a month she can take off. Tell her if she should expect a bonus on Eid, Diwali, Christmas and so on. Let her know that if there are visitors and an extra load of work, she will get a tip from them or from you. Also, if you have a 12-hour maid and you are late getting back from work or choose to go out with friends or your husband at night, give her overtime to look after your child instead of telling her that she worked a few hours less on one day 3 weeks ago and you're adjusting it now!

Martinet Mama: How to Discipline Children

Parenting is not easy—especially not at the end of a long day, when you are frustrated and tired. I've tried to discipline my children with love and care. I've been stern too, and not allowed them to get things that I've promised if they've misbehaved. I have held on to my word of giving and taking away. They know that if I'm upset I will not play with or talk to them, that I will sit very quietly. They are scared and they don't misbehave then. It takes patience to understand a child's psychology. Hitting and screaming never help. When I feel that I am so tired that I might lash out, I immediately go out for a brisk 10-minute walk to calm myself and remind myself that they are only children who are testing boundaries and are actually good-hearted souls who love me unconditionally.

You have to be mature with your children because you've had that much more experience and that much more time to acquire common sense and to develop a rational personality. You need to use your brain instead of venting your frustration.

I don't give in to them. I say things firmly. If I say, 'You can drink this milk now or in half an hour,' and the child's response is to throw the milk on the floor, I respond with: 'I'm very disappointed in you. No special playing for you today. You can leave now.' And then, even if the child starts crying, I don't hug her, no matter how much I want to. I don't give in to her bad behaviour because that would mean that she can get away with anything. Let her cry it out.

You can also use the naughty corner method. If a child is naughty, I send him to a chair or sofa that is kept in one corner of the room, away from his toys. No one talks to him for five whole minutes. And if he gets up from the chair, he is put right back into it. It's a great way to discipline children because they don't like being secluded from others.

I also believe that negotiating and bribing do not help because then the child will expect it every time. Earlier, I used to say, 'When I come back home, I'll bring you a present.' So then, even when I went for a walk, they expected me to walk back home with a present! They would be very disappointed when I didn't bring one. Kids today are so sharp that you cannot get into negotiations all the time. So I would tell them that they either listened to me or they did not get anything. In fact, if they did not listen, I would take away things they already had.

However, every time I went out of town, I did bring back something special for them. It wasn't so much out of guilt as it was to maintain a tradition. My mother used to do it for us when we were kids and I'm carrying that on with mine.

Affirmation

It's okay to leave my child in the hands of a good caregiver.
I will still take out ample time for my child
and he will always love me the most.

Accompanied Minors: Travelling with Children

Since I had both my children at Breach Candy Hospital in Mumbai, I didn't need to travel anywhere for some time after I came home. But because I love travelling, I wanted my kids to understand the idea of going and seeing new places and meeting different people very early on. So I planned family vacations where I would take my children within India and outside India to show them whole new cultures. I have travelled a lot with Samaira, on my own, even without a maid. We travelled all the way to Japan when Samaira was a year and a half. Once, I celebrated New Year's Eve with Samaira in Hong Kong—alone, minus a maid, at midnight, in a restaurant, her sleeping in her pram! It's one of my most treasured memories because I did it on my own with such a young child and I did it my way. I wanted to bond with just her and celebrate together. It was a very special New Year's Eve for me.

I learnt a few things by being a 'travelling mom'. First, every child is different. Samaira was a calm child who never cried on a plane and loved looking out of the window. Kiaan had terrible pain in his ears due to the difference in air pressure and would bawl during every take-off and landing. Managing both was a chore but when I figured out what worked, they both enjoyed it. Now, we take off to London, Goa or other places whenever the kids have vacations.

After becoming a mother, I couldn't take just any flight I wanted to. The flight timings had to agree with my children's timings. I couldn't hop on to a 7 a.m. flight because that would mean getting the children ready by 4 a.m.! Neither could I take a night flight since their bedtime is 9 p.m. and they would be very cranky if they were on a flight at that time. So I started taking afternoon flights with them.

Jet-Setting Juniors: Flying with Kids

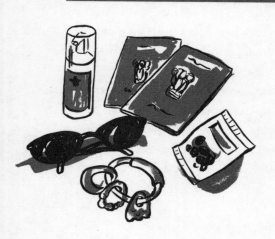

- **Ear Diary:** If you have a newborn, make him suck on a feeding bottle while taking off so that his ears don't hurt. If he has already fed and slept off, gently massage behind the base of his ear lobes to open up the ears while taking off and landing.

- **Seat Saga:** If the child is above the age limit, keep him on his own separate seat with the seat belt tightly fastened. Do not keep him on your lap, looking out of the window. It is dangerous.

- **Munch Ado:** Keep a dry snack ready at all times. Kids will feel hungry at the oddest times and you can't wait for the cart to come around every time. Also keep a bottle of clean drinking water handy. Make sure it's at room temperature for chilled water might give your child a sore throat.

- **Germ Buster:** Carry wet wipes and a hand sanitizer. Children will touch all sorts of things, including other people. You don't want those germ-laced hands going into his mouth!

- **Toy Story:** Carry a few toys that your child likes playing with. Make sure they're not too bulky. Crayons with a colouring book, some Play-Doh, a storybook you can read to him, a jigsaw puzzle or a stuffed toy will keep him busy during the waking hours in a flight. You can even carry an iPad with downloaded games or a music gadget with headphones so he can listen to music or even your laptop to show him a film or some family pictures.

- **Tiny Treats:** Do indulge your kids in little treats like cupcakes or chips. Travelling should be fun for them and they will feel more comfortable with the idea if they are pampered a bit. Make sure it's not close to their nap time though or else the sugar high might keep them awake when you don't want them to be!

- **Snug Bug:** Carry a separate fluffy blanket for your children. Many long-haul flights give out blankets but they might not be enough to keep your child warm. Shorter flights within India do not give blankets at all and it can get cold in the cabin.

- **Time Tested:** Book a flight that suits your child's timings. Night flights are a good idea since the child can just sleep through the journey. If he doesn't wake up early, don't book yourself too early in the morning. And late-night flights make it tiring for kids when they come home. It might seem like just a 2-hour flight between Mumbai and Delhi but, with my children, I have calculated that the exact time it takes us from leaving one home to reaching the other is actually about 5½ hours, what with traffic, waiting at the airport, baggage claims and the actual flight time, if it is on time!

- **Costume Drama:** Carry an extra set of clothes for your kids in your cabin baggage. If they soil the ones they are wearing, you can easily change them instead of waiting till you land and taking clothes out of your checked-in luggage. Also, carry their sunglasses. It might be sunny wherever you go and you don't want their eyes to suffer any sun damage!

- **Paperwork:** Make photocopies of all tickets, passports, visas and details like home address, important numbers, hotel reservations, etc., and keep them in a separate bag. In case you misplace the originals or your bag gets stolen, you'll still have the photocopies to show the police or the embassy if you're in a foreign country.

Usually, my vacations are for longer periods, like 2 weeks or a month, so I can plan what we'll do each day. I make sure I have hotel bookings or a place to stay before I land. If we are staying with friends, I buy a really nice present for the hosts and discipline the children a little more in their house. But, more often than not, we stay in service apartments or hotels because then we have control over when we come and go and the kids can make as much of a mess as they like. I also pack intelligently, depending on the season and weather in our destination. However, I tend to overpack because with kids I never know if they're too hot or too cold at any time.

Tots on Trips: Travelling with Kids

- **Pace It Out:** Remember that you'll need to take it quite slow. If you could once do the hectic backpacking through Europe—you know those whirlwind trips where you visit twenty-one countries in twenty-one days—now you can probably do a few cities at best in the same time. Children will feel hungry, cranky and sleepy at exactly the time the tour is ready to leave. So give yourself and your kids some leeway to enjoy places at leisure.

- **Plan Ahead:** Plan your vacation well in advance and make an itinerary for each day of your vacation. You know when the kids have holidays since the school gives out the calendar at the beginning of the year. Plan and book hotels and flights as early as you can so you are not stressed about where to go a week before the vacations commence!

- **Plan Smart:** Check in advance if you can get discounts at particular places for family. Most hotels offer special family packages and it becomes more economical.

- **Pack the Basics:** Carry medicines, Band-Aids, paracetamol, daily vitamins, cotton and your children's health cards when on a vacation. You never know when they'll catch a cold or a fever or cut themselves. Then, running around by yourself to find a pharmacy for small things can be quite cumbersome. Trim the kids' nails before you travel and carry the nail-cutter in your checked-in luggage. Within a week, you'll see the kids' nails growing out and a simple nail-cutter can be expensive in a foreign land.

• **Follow the Rules:** If you're going to a country that requires particular immunizations, get all the vaccinations done on time. Ask your travel agent and cross-check online or with the consulate about the country's entry rules, lest you land up at the airport and are denied entry!

• **Change Money:** Keep enough foreign currency of the country you're travelling to. You might need to pay for cabs or buy something at the airport and if they don't accept credit cards, you could be stuck.

• **Take a Pram:** If your child is less than 6 years old, carry a pram. You can always check it in when you're boarding but walking long distances or carrying the child in your arms through different airports can get rather tiring.

• **Carry It All:** Bring your own feeding bottles, sterilizer, baby food, toys, nappy rash creams, wet wipes, medicines, milk formula, etc. Airlines will not give any of this to you.

• **Manage Your Luggage:** Carry a midsize strolley. You don't want to struggle with managing children as well as an overloaded suitcase or overflowing backpack! By the time you reach your destination, your back would have given way. Carry a set of clothes for each kid in the hand baggage. If they get anything wet or dirty, you have a change ready for them.

• **Hydrate the Kids:** Give the children water, juice or soup frequently through the flight to avoid any chances of dehydration due to the cabin pressure.

I remember when I travelled by train for the first time. I was around five years old and I loved the trees whooshing past. I wanted to give my children the same experience. Since Kiaan is still quite young, I have not let him travel by train but Samaira has. She enjoys the sound of the train as it thumps away while your body finds a groove with the movement.

Railway Children: Train Trips with Kids

• **Space Story:** If you're travelling as a large family and you've got all or several compartments to yourself, then you can be comfortable. If, however, there's only one or two of you travelling, ensure that you give each other space by managing the luggage and sitting area, and allow your child to play only in a designated area that you can control.

• **Extra Seats:** It is smarter to buy extra seats so you can have more space and privacy. Rail travel in India allows children under the age of 4 to travel free but I would suggest you book an extra berth so that you can sleep comfortably and the child has space to play as well on her berth.

• **Food Fundas:** Carry your own food. You may not want to eat the food the train provides. By packing your own snacks, you're assured of the nutritive quality and hygiene. Carry juice, water, fruit, biscuits, sandwiches and any other eatables that the child particularly likes.

• **Fun Time:** Make sure the child has enough to do, since train journeys can take several hours. You need to keep kids occupied with playing cards, a small ball, tic-tac-toe board, Play-Doh, puzzles, action figures or colouring books. You can also walk around and let your baby find new friends.

• **Comfy Outfits:** Wear comfortable clothes. It's going to be a long journey. Making kids wear fancy dresses or tight clothes will only cause you misery when they start howling. Let them wear comfortable trackpants or tights or stretchable shorts with loose cotton shirts. You can always layer them with a sweater or jacket and add socks when you reach your destination. Make sure you and your children wear slip-on shoes, which are easy to slip off when you are seated and easy to slip on when you need to go to the bathroom or just walk about.

• **Staying Alert:** Be careful about whom you leave your kids with. If you're taking one child to the toilet, make sure the other understands that he should stay put. You can even think about tying a little *ghungroo* or bell to the child's hand or leg so you can hear where they are at all times. Never let your children out of your sight.

• **Keeping Watch:** Be careful of children playing on the railings or hanging out of trains. Don't leave them unsupervised. Be watchful of what they do if they're roaming around by themselves.

• **Route Plan:** Take your time getting on and getting off. To disembark, don't pick a station that has only a 2-minute stoppage. You have to mind your step with kids while you're managing your bag as well as your luggage. If it's a short halt, you'll be rushed and anything can happen.

• **Packing Right:** Don't overpack. Just because it's a train, don't think you can carry two large suitcases with two small suitcases and add a basket of mangoes for your favourite aunt. The more luggage you have, the more you will have to worry. Fruit can be flown in by courier but your children will need all your attention during the trip—you can't have your mind wandering off to count whether all your suitcases and bags and baskets are near you!

Carry your own toiletries and other basics. I have listed the essential ones below:

Mommy's Essential Travel Tote

- Toothpaste, toothbrush (for overnight trips)
- Talcum powder
- Toilet paper
- Hand sanitizer
- Soap strips or liquid-soap dispenser
- Small napkin to wipe your face
- Small towel to wipe your hands
- Paper tissues to wipe hands and blow noses
- Moisturizer
- Mosquito repellent ointment or spray
- Laundry soap (should you need to quickly wash anything that gets soiled)
- Torch and batteries
- Chargers and converters for phones and other gizmos
- Suntan or sun block
- Sunglasses for kids
- Safety pins
- Band-Aids
- Paracetamol for kids
- Raincoats or umbrella
- Oh, and a camera to capture all the wonderful moments!

When you have all these, you can stop fretting about your children's hygiene and comfort, and enjoy your vacation!

Whenever I travelled by train, I met very interesting people and many children became friends with Samaira. I had an emergency stash of small chocolates to distribute and everyone appreciated the effort. You see, journeys are calorie-free! Most people who are on a diet or workout regimen feel that while they are travelling, they don't need to watch their weight—the hours of moving burn it all up! But I always carry healthy food for myself and enough indulgences, like parathas, theplas, sandwiches and cookies, for my children and for those around me. People are more pleasant after having been fed a nice treat. That's my trick to happy journeys!

I haven't written about parents travelling with differently abled or special children—I don't know what the exact procedures are, though the tips I have given above would help during any kind of travel. Don't hesitate to ask your travel agent or the railway or airline officials to make special provisions for you and your child, give you priority boarding, arrange for a wheelchair or provide any other assistance you need to make it a pleasant trip. You should make the journey and the vacation as wonderful for you and your child as possible instead of taking on all the small details yourself. Bon voyage!

Affirmation

I will have a great time with my children.
I will not stress them or myself out over small details.
It's a vacation after all!

The Chronicles of Mama Mia

Of Helping Children Grow and Growing along with Them

Tuesdays with Karisma: A Day in the Life of a Superstar

Whether he is 3 months old or 3 years old, your child must have a routine. As must you. It is very important indeed. Here is my routine with my children:

7 a.m.
Wake up, have a glass of hot water, wake up the children

7.15 a.m.
Have a cup of coffee, get Samaira ready for school

8 a.m.
Drop Samaira to school, have breakfast, read the papers or check my to-do list for the day

9 a.m.
Get Kiaan ready for school, sit with him to have some fruit

10 a.m.
Drop Kiaan to school, head for yoga

10.15 a.m.
Do an intense 1-hour yoga session

11.15 a.m.
Eat some fruit, head for a nice, long shower for my muscles to relax

Noon
Head for my fittings and meetings

1 p.m.
Pick the kids up from school

1.30 p.m.
Have lunch with the kids at the dining table, chat about what they did in school

2 p.m.
Make Kiaan sleep, read a book with Samaira or help her with homework

4 p.m.
Wake Kiaan up, have an evening snack (fruit, poha, upma) with both kids

4.15 p.m.
Drop kids to respective lessons (art, dance, judo, kathak, tae kwon do, swimming)

4.30–7.30 p.m.
Go for meetings, script sessions, etc.

7.30 p.m.–8 p.m.
Have dinner with the kids, hear a wrap-up of their activities

8–9 p.m.
Make the kids brush their teeth, change into pyjamas, read to them, pray with them, make them sleep

9 p.m.–Midnight
Me time! Finally, watch some TV and catch up on all the American shows I love!

When you structure the day and plan a routine for your children, you'll realize that you also automatically fall into it. My schedule obviously changes when I'm on a shoot, for then I leave early in the morning and come back only when the shoot is done. For those days, I arrange for my children to visit me in the evening after their afternoon nap so I can still catch up with them, despite my work.

I've noticed that mealtimes become quite fixed. Children like to wake up in the morning and have a glass of milk. If they're feeling too lazy in the morning, then I carry some breakfast along in the car while dropping them to school. It's usually something dry like an egg sandwich, whereas at home they would have porridge or toast.

I've also noticed that setting the routine for your second child is much easier than for the first. The second one just follows what the first one does and automatically wants to copy everything. So if you've got it pat down with the first kid, the second one will come easy. Younger children pick up things much faster because they intuitively learn from the elder sibling while also instinctively competing with him! I've forbidden TV watching in my house, except on weekends, so Kiaan never even mentions it. But he knows all about Spiderman, Superman and the Hulk because of older cousins and our extended family.

I have learnt not to take afternoon naps. My body needs only 6–7 hours of sleep at night. However, women who can take power naps in the afternoon should do so for 20–30 minutes to feel refreshed and energized to play with their children.

It's also important to engage your children in different, interesting activities. My son goes for football, dance and storytime while my daughter has lessons in kathak, painting and swimming. Younger children need fewer activities but more play dates where they can interact with other children of their age. It is only now that I have started mingling with the mothers of my kids' classmates. Now I also send the kids over to their friends' houses and have their friends over at ours. Earlier, I would take them to meet my friends' kids. But ever since Samaira made her own social circle, it is important for me to get to know the parents and interact more. I think it's very nice because I've made a whole new set of friends that I would not ordinarily have had. I have a great bond with these mothers. We can share so many different things that I can't with my single friends.

Mama Drama: Bonding with Other Moms

- **Open Your Mind:** Not everyone is going to have the same sensibilities as you. If your child is close to a woman's daughter/son, you need to make an effort to know that person. You will probably not have much in common but be flexible and talk about different things for the sake of your child. If you're shy, start befriending one or two people and sharing a cup of coffee with them. Gradually, if you want, you can expand your group.

- **Splurge a Bit:** If you're taking your child over for a play date, pack tiffin for your child so the other mother is not hassled about what to feed your child. You can also take a small treat for the mom and her kids, like cupcakes, muffins or some sandwiches that they can all have later.

- **Make a Group:** From your yoga class and your children's school to the park and the library—you can find mothers everywhere. Make your own small group and have those children and mothers come over occasionally. That way, your child can have a set of new friends.

- **Stay In, Go Out:** If you have a small house or are fussy about too many children being at home, you can take them out. So, once a month, you can take all the play date children for a movie where they can enjoy snacks and spend a few hours together without getting your house dirty. That way you can feel less guilty about not calling them over and yet send your child when there is a play date at someone else's home.

- **Plan It Out:** Many working moms do not have time to bond on weekdays. You can take them out for a quick cup of coffee or a drink after work to bond. Stay-at-home moms also have several chores they need to finish during the week. It would be nice if you could take them out for a spa occasionally. They'll feel much obliged and take good care of your children when they go over to their house.

Frankly, when Samaira was younger, I used to find it a bit difficult to bond with mothers because certain people would understandably look at me differently, as if they were thinking, 'Oh, she is a movie star! Will she be friendly?' But when they got to know me, a lot of moms would say, 'You're so normal' or 'You're so chilled out' and I would go, 'Yeah, I'm just like you and I'm going through the same experiences as you.' With Kiaan's friends' moms, though, I have opened up a lot more and a lot quicker. It has been much easier the second time around.

I have also noticed that some mothers have this sense of competition about losing weight or looking good. I think it's an unhealthy road to go on. Everyone has a different metabolism and different lifestyle so we should never compare ourselves with others. When we stop comparing, we start living better.

So now, I'm part of a huge group of moms. We all have our individual problems and solutions, and we help each other. At times, we just listen to each other—that helps a lot too. Having someone to crib to and bond with gives me tremendous joy.

Affirmation

Making new friends is a boon.
My circle expands to include people who will help me.
I will support my child by having a healthy
relationship with his friends' parents.

Tricks of the Trade: Of Shopping, Crèches and Bonding

Shopping for Kids and with Kids

I love dressing up my daughter! I have to admit that from the time she was a baby, I would go shopping for different dresses, shoes, clips, hairbands, and do all sorts of dressing up. She was my little doll and I loved it. Now, Samaira has reached the stage where she says, 'But Mom, I want to wear this!' So it is a bit of a negotiation between us but I am particular about what my kids should or should not wear. I'm a bit of a conservative mom. I know it may sound really silly in today's time but I may not send my daughter everywhere in shorts even though she is so young; I feel those are the things that my mom brought us up with and I want to continue doing them. I feel I've made my own little fashion icon and set her free into the world. With my son, it's very different. He hardly cares about what he wears as long as he wears it quickly. The buttons cannot be fussed over and there are jeans, shorts, shirts. That's it. No hair accessories.

No pretty pink shoes. And definitely no cute belts, hairbands and bows. So I'm lucky to have had the best of both worlds.

I take Samaira along when I go shopping. With girls, it's really fun and I think it's a good bonding exercise for moms, especially when girls are between 4 and 8 years old. I even get my clothes coordinated with my daughter's, so we have a few photos of us dressed up in the same thing. She thinks it's hilarious and I feel so close to her that way. Kiaan is still young but when I do take him shopping, I give him the option to choose. He would come up to me, even when he was barely 2 years old, and say, 'Mama, I want this!'

Hollywood celebrity moms have to deal with a lot more pressure than we do in Bollywood. The paparazzi there scrutinize everyone and everything. So they will be looking at what Angelina Jolie's kids are wearing and compare it to Katie Holmes's kids. Honestly, children should be left alone. Women have enough pressure on them, balancing careers and homes, and they should not be worrying about whether they should buy designer wear for their kids so the photographers can't give them hell! Each to her own, really. We should respect each individual and their homes, their financial capacities and so on. At the end of the day, it is your child and not something you entered in a competition. Give him what you can afford; never feel pressurized to do more. I want to tell all you moms and dads out there that there is no pressure and you know best what you can afford for your child, what you can give your child and what you want to give your child. You may be able to buy him anything under the sun or you may not want to give those values to your child—it's your child, your call.

How does it really matter if your kid is wearing mismatched clothes when he has a great personality? Be proud of your children for who they are and not what others make them out to be. I don't buy brands for my children often. I've seen 3-year-olds dressed in Burberry and Dior. I shop on Hill Road, Bandra, and Mothercare and Green Bell in Juhu if I'm in Mumbai and from Greater Kailash market and regular malls when I'm in Delhi. Sometimes, I might pick up a branded outfit if I feel it's a special occasion like a birthday. Also, I've probably chosen an outfit once in a while for the extra bit of quality or design that I haven't found anywhere else.

Ageless Allure: Glam at Any Age

I love coordinating my clothes with my children's for occasions like Christmas or Diwali. Last year, for a traditional party, I wore a magenta salwar-kameez, Samaira wore a similar kurta (and the same bangles as mine) and Kiaan wore a white kurta embroidered in magenta. We looked so cute! For Christmas, if Kiaan wears a tuxedo, Samaira and I wear coordinated dresses. It makes the kids feel more bonded with me. Also, I think women can be glamorous at any age. You just need to put in a little effort.

The XXXX Factor: Go Glam in Your Forties!

- Keep your metabolic rate high. Eat intelligently, exercise consciously.
- Dress age appropriately. Wear a short dress, yes, but redefine short: should it end just above your knees rather than just below your bum? Gain the respect of your teenage kid.
- Pair a well-fitting pair of jeans with a crisply starched pretty blouse—the ensemble looks glam at any age.
- Don't go overboard with jewellery; wear one statement piece. Pearls are elegant but save them for your fifties. And forget the funky-chunky accessories of your twenties. Diamonds, of course, are forever!
- A scarf can be a stunning accessory, especially in bright silks, in winters.
- High heels keep you young so invest in some stilettos, some peep toes!
- Avoid belts unless you have washboard abs.
- Wear understated make-up. Perfect base, touch of gloss, some kajal—and you're all set.

• Wear sunscreen during the day and moisturize your skin well. Hydration prevents wrinkles. Use an anti-ageing night cream.

Ageing gracefully is an art. Whether you dye your hair or stay grey, be confident of who you are. Don't give up on life and yourself just because you're done having children. Stay healthy, stay gorgeous. It's not about whether your husband still cares! It's about how good you feel about yourself. Life is a gift. Live it well.

Mall Brats: Kid-Friendly Shopping Ideas

• **Grocery Super-Marts:** If you've gone shopping with your children, seat them in a big shopping cart while you pick up things. That way, you have your eyes on them at all times. Do not leave the cart unattended in any situation.

• **Outfits:** Make sure they wear something comfy and snug. You don't want to dress them up in fancy clothes that will get dirty. Write their names and your mobile number on the labels of their clothes so that in case they get lost in the market someone can contact you. Give your child a whistle to wear around his neck; if someone tries any hanky-panky, they can whistle and attract your attention. But tell them not to whistle unnecessarily or there will be a huge racket!

• **Sales:** Skip the big sales when you have two or more kids. The stores are packed with people and it's difficult to manoeuvre and find the correct sizes for the children. Go to places that are not overflowing with people on that day.

• **Numbers:** Make sure your child knows your name and phone number in case he gets lost and someone asks him. If he can't remember your name, he probably shouldn't be let out of the stroller to stroll around without supervision.

• **Security Areas:** Show your kid where to go in case he gets lost. A security guard or policeman, a store owner or other authorized personnel like mall concierges can help your children. You can also tell the guards operating the store doors that your child shouldn't be allowed to leave without your supervision.

• **Known Areas:** Do not go alone to areas you yourself are unfamiliar with. If you've visited the place before, you can take your children there. You don't want to be running around frantically, trying to find your children who are playing in places you're uncomfortable in.

- **Shopping Mates:** If you go with a fellow mom, she can take the boys to figure out outfits while you can take the daughters to figure out their sizes and so on. This way you don't have to cover everything.

- **Strollers:** All kids under the age of 5 get tired from walking in malls for more than 20 minutes. Bring a stroller so they can sit while you check out stuff.

- **Food:** All children feel hungry at the oddest times. Carry a healthy snack like a sandwich so they don't crave junk food. After you're done, you can give them a small treat from the food court.

- **Timing:** If you want to buy groceries AND pick clothes AND check out household items, it is best to go alone. When you're with children, stick to one thing and just do that in a day. They will get tired and cranky and you will get annoyed and irritated if you can't complete your chores.

Shopping can be very tiring for parents. The children will forever be demanding toys or food or something else that catches their fancy. They will want to be carried. They will want to run in the aisles. You have to keep your sanity about you. Learn to say no to many things and not feel guilty. Before you go to a store, remind them that they can pick out only one thing and eat only one goody treat. Be firm and don't give in to their demands. If you feel they're getting out of hand, put them in the stroller and take them aside to give them a warning. If the situation gets out of hand, I suggest you leave the shopping area without buying them anything and get back home. You can always go back later by yourself or with them but you need to make sure they understand you mean business.

Another thing, hunger can make you more frazzled. So eat before you leave. Or take a break while shopping to have a cup of coffee and a quick bite. Keep a separate day only for shopping, instead of trying to fit in many things in that one day. If you've chosen a weekend, ask a friend or your husband to help with the kids while you go around picking things up. Take turns while managing your time with the children and buying things.

The most important tip that I can give you about shopping with children is to MAKE A LIST! Carry the list with you so you don't wander aimlessly through aisles. Stick to the list and get things done quickly.

Whether it is shopping or playing, spending time with your children is extremely important. I make it a point to drop my children to school and pick them up. I think kids love to see their parents at the end of a long day at school. We chat on the way home about what happened in school and we get to bond.

In the evenings, we all play Monopoly, Housie and other board games. Of course, these are for children aged 5 and above. With Kiaan, I join his play with all his action figurines and we make up stories and noises. He loves animals so he has these little figures of animals that he loves playing with; it's good because he also gets to learn about animals, words, colours and so on. You can also give them books to read, make them hear good music and dance to it. Kiaan dances to everything from nursery rhymes to Bollywood *gaanas*.

Crèches, Schools and Quality Time

Many working parents leave their children in crèches. I have never done so but I have many friends who have. In such cases, I think it becomes far more important to spend quality time with your children every day, without fail. You can't have other people bringing up your children and you only hearing about their growth from strangers. Even if you get only a few hours in the evening with your children, make sure you switch off your phone and laptop and spend every minute with your child bonding over what he's done and what he's learnt. Ask her pertinent questions that she can answer instead of general ones like what she did. Ask her what she ate and if she liked it, what her best friend and she did together, how she shared something with the group, which colour she used to paint and so on. Whatever time you get to spend with the child, make it last and make it count.

Home Away from Home: Finding a Good Crèche

- **Close to Home:** You need to find a crèche close to home so you can pick up the child on the way home, or send a maid or family member to pick the child up and not worry about how far away they are.

- **Clean and Clear:** Check the play areas and bathrooms. They must be clean and hygienic. Your child will spend a few hours at the place and you don't want any germs to spread or your child to fall ill. Floors, corridors, walls and the kitchen area must be spotless; rubbish bins should not be left overflowing. The toilets should be clean and hygienic, and ideally customized for young children. Playing equipment should also be cleaned regularly and maintained well.

- **Good Staff:** Make sure the teachers and assistants are well qualified to look after your child and are themselves conscious of hygiene. A qualified, dedicated and professional staff which is good with children is a must for a good crèche. I don't recommend a crèche with male staff. And even with women, too much kissing and cuddling should never be encouraged.

- **Learning:** Make sure the crèche doesn't put on TV the whole day long for your child. It should have specific activities for the kids every day, and these can range from educational to free play. The crèche should value creativity and facilitate a lot of drawing, painting, sports, dance and music that the kids can enjoy individually and as a group.

- **Food:** If the crèche gives food, make sure you go and sample it beforehand. If you can, try to see the process and the place where it is being made so you can be assured of the cleanliness. Else, send snacks with your child to eat every 2 hours. Make sure there's enough in case the child wants to share it with her friends. Also send a bottle of fresh water. Check if the crèche has clean drinking water in case her bottle gets over.

- **Medical Checks:** The crèche should have a doctor on call and a first-aid kit handy at all times. Also check if they know what to do in case a child chokes, gets a cut, is stung by a bee and so on.

- **Ventilation:** See if there are enough fans, air conditioners and windows for proper ventilation. Also check if they can handle power cuts and have a generator or inverter for essentials.

- **Electrical Sockets:** Tell them to baby-proof the lower-positioned electrical sockets if you're leaving very young children at the crèche.

- **Safety Precautions:** If there are many children of different ages, then there should be staff to deal with them separately. There should be baby chairs for younger kids to eat meals in. There should be stair gates if the crèche is in a duplex house. The nap areas should be separate, with baby monitors. Balconies will need to be cordoned off.

- **Picking Up Kids:** The crèche should send kids off only with the parents or the staff that the parents have authorized. The kids should not be entrusted to anyone else, unless you have specified so. If you're going to be late for picking up your child, call them in advance. Personally, I feel that no child should be left unsupervised with just a driver or male staff at any point in time.

I know that many fathers are unable to figure out how to spend quality time with their children. They might have picked out the best crèche and even found great babysitters but when it comes to actually spending time with their kids, they seem to be rather lost. A few working mothers also feel the same way. I think children need your time more than anything. You don't need to do anything fancy with them to bond. Give them as much attention as you can. When Samaira was a year old, I took her on a trip to Hong Kong. I spent

New Year's Eve with her there in a restaurant and saw the fireworks and we really bonded. She might not remember it but I know that it was very important for me.

Family Ties: Bonding with Your Kids

• **Take Vacations:** There's nothing better than taking your children on a vacation where you don't have to worry about domestic life and they can have fun with you. Whether it is a road trip or a flight to some place else, a break from the routine always helps you bond better. If you cannot get away from the city, all you need to do is plan a picnic. Take a basket full of goodies and playthings to a city garden, and sit there, eating and chatting and playing and reading!

• **Eat Together:** Many people eat their meals in front of the TV set. Make sure you all sit together at the dining table for even 10 minutes while you're eating and talk about food and what you're eating and cooking. Children can tell you about the vegetables they like and you can tell them about the goodness in even the vegetables they do not like.

• **Read Together:** Every day, take out time to read a few pages from a book with your kids. Talk to them about the stories or poems or the characters in the tales. Teach them a new word every day. Ask them what they learnt from what they read. Reading together is a great way to bond.

• **Work and Homework:** Sit and do something of your own while the kids do their homework. If it's a special project like a collage, help them. If you sit with them every day for a little while when they're doing their homework, it encourages them to focus, ask for assistance and strike up conversations.

• **Make-Believe:** Make a little fort in the house with some cushions and sheets and pretend you're soldiers in a battle. Take face paint and colour each other's faces and pretend you are clowns. Wear some old clothes and cut up some dupattas to make saris or smaller dupattas and pretend you are Bollywood heroines and dance around. What fun!

• **Clean and Sort:** Help the kids clean out their drawers and cabinets and ask them which playthings they like best. You might uncover some hidden treasures that your child might like playing with again. And he'll learn to keep things sorted, organized and clean!

- **Cook Together:** With children older than 6, you can cook, bake, grill and chop together. Making a meal for the family that everyone can enjoy later will give the child immense pleasure and a sense of ownership.

- **Sing Out Loud:** This idea works with younger children as well. Sing a song and tell them to sing it with you, or ask them to sing one that they like or have learnt in school. The one with the most number of songs wins. Obviously you never keep score and they always win; you can give them a small treat at the end. Babies and infants love hearing you sing as well. It doesn't matter if you're out of tune. It's the smile on your face they respond to.

- **Out and About:** Take your children to museums, aquariums, parks, baby gyms, zoos, playgrounds, etc. Anything outdoors will help you bond as you do fun things together and as you watch them grow and interact with other people.

- **Maintain Traditions:** Don't let go of family traditions like praying, celebrating Diwali and Holi, and so on, where the whole family gets together or you perform a particular ritual. Start a new tradition if you want, like taking the children to a temple on the first Saturday of every month or taking pizza holidays where you go to a kids' area in a mall and have pizzas with the family. Or you can plant a tree or do something with plants in a botanical garden once a month. By sticking to something, you can show them the importance of nurturing a tradition that connects the family.

Affirmation

I need to make time now for my child before
it's too late and he doesn't need me.
I have so many things to learn as a parent.
I'm doing the best I can.

Kindergarten Cop: Dealing with School Issues

Playschool can be a very traumatic time for a mother and her child. In fact, I think it is the second most traumatic phase after the delivery. Going to that school and hearing your child howling away and leaving him all alone among new people, new children and new teachers is the worst experience you can have, especially if you have a weepy child. The angst of leaving him alone will have you crying buckets!

I cried for a year. One whole year. No jokes. Actually, Samaira took very long to settle in so I would literally be sitting outside for those two hours, shaking and not knowing what was going on—it was literally like a Hindi movie scene. Samaira was very shy. Also, she would see other kids cry and start crying—kids do tend to start howling because other children are howling. I sat outside because they would not allow me to sit inside the school. So I would either hang out outside or in the car, or drive around for a bit and come back. I was so traumatized!

In retrospect, I was quite silly. It was not the end of the world. Kids settle down eventually and end up loving school. So hang in there. As for Kiaan, touch wood, he just walked in and settled down. There may have been a few days here and there with a few sniffles but he loved playschool overall. So I have had both experiences. There was a bit of anxiety on my part though—I would wonder how he would be in there, but I was very lucky with him.

I think the most challenging thing for mothers is the tiffin. In my house, we follow a system of specific snacks on specific days of the week. The system works because then neither the cook nor the mom is confused about what to make and send every morning. In the mad rush of waking up the children and getting them ready, the last thing you want to worry about is what tiffin to make! I would advise that you give them healthy snacks as often as possible. Occasionally, give in to their demands for goodies. Now, Samaira is at an age where she says what she likes and wants.

Our Tiffin Days

Monday
Chocolate sandwich/peanut butter and jelly sandwich/salami and cheese sandwich

Tuesday
Aloo parantha/gobhi parantha/vegetable cutlets/soy tikkis

Wednesday
Poha/upma/mini idlis with butter and chutney/dhoklas/fresh dosas/theplas

Thursday

Chicken nuggets/egg sandwich/hummus with pita bread/potato smileys

Friday

Pasta with garlic bread/cheese sandwich and popcorn/raw or bolied vegetables/boiled eggs

On most days, I also add a small box of fruit, like cut apple or small chunks of watermelon without seeds or a banana. Other days, I send nuts like cashews, raisins, walnuts and almonds with some crunchy muesli so that they can snack on something if they're not too full. I also give them a small box of cereal every day, in case they want to eat something sweet. I try and make the food exciting and different so they don't get bored.

You must make everything fresh in the morning. If you're sending leftovers, they must only be from dinner the previous night, say pasta or some wedges of a pizza. Don't send anything older than that. It may go bad and give your child an upset stomach.

To and Fro: Transport System

Luckily, I can afford to send my children to school in a car. Many schools insist on kids being sent by bus but I'm a little sceptical of buses for younger children. I would like my children to travel by school bus when they turn 9 or 10 so that they can experience it—it's an amazing place to bond with the children of your neighbourhood; I know because I went to school in a bus. It also teaches kids to be independent. Do make sure, though, that there is always a teacher or an ayah or a maid in the bus. Obviously, you should tell your child not to walk around in a moving bus, not to hit and slap children or get into fights. Children who go by car must sit in the back with their seat belts fastened. I never allow my children to sit in the front seat, not even for a short spin; if you allow that one time, then they will be on your case forever! My personal opinion is, and no offence to anyone, that you must never send your children alone with the driver. In today's time, whether it is a girl child or a boy child, it is a big no-no. There is no question on earth of letting a child accompany the driver or even a security guard in the elevator alone. There should be you, or a maid and driver, or a grandparent with them. Also, if a child is going on a long-distance journey like a school trip, please see that there is somebody responsible travelling with him.

Card Code: School Security

It's really a good thing that every school, whether it is a nursery or a formal school, has an identity card system now. Security in schools has become really amazing and that is one thing parents don't need to worry about because the school authorities don't let the child leave unless you don't show them the card with all the relevant pictures on it.

School Daze: Some Rituals

Every year, before school begins, we have a family ritual of going and buying new water bottles, tiffin boxes, shoes, socks and other things needed for school. We make a whole fun day out of it so they can look forward to new things and the ritual sets them up for a good first day at school as well. Some things get used up pretty quickly or get lost, so we go every 2 months and the kids pick up matching things.

Academic Rigour: Picking a Good School

Whichever school you pick, make sure it has trained staff, clean toilets, and plenty of play areas. You want your child to develop overall instead of just being a rote learner. See that the teacher–student ratio is kept to a minimum so that they give enough individual attention to your child. Also see that there are plenty of extracurricular activities to keep your child busy. Music, elocution, fine motor skills and sports are important. For toddlers, see if they allow children who are not potty-trained. Go by your instinct when picking a school rather than putting your child into a fancy school where everyone in your friends' circle sends their kids. They can meet their friends after school but their education needs to be thorough and sound, from the very beginning.

How to Spark Your Child's Imagination

Ages 3–5

Surprise them with unexpected toys. Grab a pile of household things—spoons, cotton balls, toilet paper rolls—and toss them on to the middle of the floor. For more novelty, mix in some toys that are normally kept in a different room. See what they can imagine and create!

Create an obstacle course. In the backyard or at the park, set up a fun obstacle course. How about this? Swing once on the swing, hop five times, run in a circle, then make a little sculpture with leaves. Then let your child set up his own course that you and others must follow.

Ages 6–9

Act it out. Suggest that your child and his siblings or friends perform a play or TV show. Give them paper to make tickets, set a time when you'll be available to watch, then let them get to rehearsals. (And don't set up a stage; they'll figure that out themselves. And the props. And the script!)

Ages 9–11

Create a game. Pull out all the family games and suggest that your child create his own, either using all original materials or pulling ideas and props from existing games. Suggest that he write down the rules, and agree to play with him when he's done.

How to Really Read Books

Every child loves books, and every parent loves having a child who reads, for they'll do well in school. But books and stories are also a great source of creative fun. When children learn, they have the ability to take stories off the page and they feel empowered to let their own amazing ideas take over. Children of almost any age have the ability to compose their own tales—all you need to do is encourage them.

Ages 3–6

Listen and learn. Start by telling your preschooler stories. Anything that comes to mind—a personal story inspired by a book or a tale of your own childhood or some fantastic yarn that jumps into your imagination. Start with little tales. As you're reading a story, say one about a turtle, suggest to your child that she tell you what the turtle did the next day, or what she thinks happens after the story ends.

Ages 6–9

Imagine a story. Give your child a character, object and place and let her create the story. You can also get your child to write her story down and illustrate it later. To really make her feel proud, collect a few of these stories she has penned and print out a little book, turning her into an author of sorts!

Ages 9–11

Play with stories. Your child is bound to have a favourite book or two, so have her take that story off the page. Let her create a costume for her favourite character, host a theme party based on the story or just have a dinner with food inspired by the tale.

You must nurture your children's talents and help them grow. Don't force any activity on the child but a few gentle nudges in the right direction can be helpful. I had a friend whose daughter hated going for singing lessons. Yet, after she learnt a few notes and a song, she loved the idea. So, the mom arranged for a private tutor to help her at home a few days a week.

Star Pupil: Five Ways to Help Kids Succeed in School

1. **Set a Routine:** If you have a particular homework time for the children then, no matter what, make sure that they sit and do their homework at that time on weekdays. You need to sit with them, if you have the time, to assist them with their queries. Let them sit for at least half an hour every day and do not allow them to get up till they finish. Samaira used to want to go to the bathroom every time we sat down so I made it a point that she went before we started!

2. **Be Positive:** Even if they do badly in a few areas, do not scold them. Encourage and praise them when they do well in other subjects. Find out why they're stumbling and help them. Get a tutor if you can't help in particular subjects. (Don't leave them alone with a tutor though. Make sure someone is in the room with the tutor and your child at all times. Keep the door to the room they are in open.)

3. All Support, No Excuses: 'Some people just don't have a head for math,' a parent told me once. I just don't believe it. Your child will start to think that you think she isn't able to handle a task, and she will make excuses. Success in a future job will require your child to do the best she can. You will not help her by encouraging her to make excuses whenever convenient. Let her finish her project. You shouldn't be completing it for her. A child needs to know that it's not okay to leave things undone. If she gets a bad grade for it, remind her to do it properly the next time. This way, she won't rely on you for everything and you'll be raising a responsible student.

4. Trick or Treat: Sometimes, and I specify, only *sometimes*, you should give special treats if the children have done something exceptionally well. If they've completed a project all by themselves and got a good grade or if they've got an A or a B after getting Cs and Ds in a particular subject, take them out for a special dinner or buy them something they've wanted for a long time. It encourages them more than just words and hugs.

5. Correct Place: Let your child sit at a table and do his homework instead of in front of the TV or with music playing in the background. Make sure the study area is well illuminated and bright so that he feels happy to sit down for that time.

Besides helping with schoolwork, you must encourage your child to make new friends in school. Read to them every night so that they are encouraged to go to the library in their school. Praise your children at home and help them become confident human beings. Listen to them every night, ask them what they like in school, who their friends are, what subjects are difficult or what they like doing most. My favourite time of the day is when we chat about school. I listen to their problems and they tell me about all the new things that they've accomplished.

Red Alert

Keep a close eye on your kids when they become too reticent. If older children are being bullied, they might not confide in you. Also, you must get their eyes checked every 6 months from the age of 4 years onwards. If they need glasses, you have to encourage them to wear them regularly and keep them clean. Look out for signs if they mix up letters and find it tough to write. Check if a child is dyslexic, so that you can handle him in the appropriate manner. If the child's teacher complains about him being disruptive in class, talk to him and take him out of that particular class for some time or have him transferred to another section. Find out from a counsellor why he behaves in a particular way. If going to school every day is a continuous battle, see if you can take him out and put him in another school after some time.

Make sure that going to school and learning new things are fun activities for your children. They are going to be the future leaders of our society and you want them to have well-rounded personalities.

Affirmation
I will never compare my child with another.
Every child is unique.
I will nurture my child's talents and praise him often.

Out and About: Birthday Parties and Etiquette in Public Places

Nowadays, kids' birthday parties are like mini weddings! Samaira's first birthday was a big blowout. We hosted it in the lawns of our Delhi house and the entire family was there. Because it was our first child and we wanted to do something special, we had arranged for everything we could. From balloon decorations in her name to magicians, a big cake and catered food, we didn't leave anything out. And today, she doesn't even remember it!

When Bebo and I were children, we had simple parties with some patties, sandwiches, wafers, some chips and a 1 kg cake with our name on it. We played pin-the-tail-on-the-donkey and musical chairs and everyone went home with a smile. Now, there are grand themes for birthday parties where kids come in costumes, magicians come to entertain them, a tattoo artist is called to paint action figures on their hands, specialized birthday cakes are ordered and everyone goes home with return presents that cost more than the actual party!

It's sheer madness. If you've sent your child for one party and he's come back with an expensive 'back present' and participated in all the games, then you feel you must throw a party to call his friends and return the favour. And so begins the never-ending cycle. You have a pool party and then a fairy-tale theme party and then a Disneyland theme party and it goes on . . . So much money is spent on birthday parties that you feel a huge dent in your bank account.

I finally stopped. For Kiaan's first birthday, I had a small and intimate affair at home with just family and close friends. We had such a blast because only familiar faces were present and there was less stress. I had to stop being the overindulgent mother that I was. We give our kids the best values, we give them a lot of time and we spend on their education—I don't think we need to go overboard with parties!

It is better to keep it small for the first and second birthdays. By the time he turns 3, your child may be telling you the kind of party he wants! But you should feel no pressure because there is no competition. Do what you feel is right for you and for your child. If you want to overindulge, spend a lot of money, have a wedding kind of party and if you feel happy doing that, then do that without any guilt. If you want to have a small party at home or at a club with ten or twenty kids, do that. Don't feel guilty either way. This year, Samaira had only twenty girls at her party, and Kiaan had his closest buddies.

If you do not want to have a big party but your kids have attended big parties and you feel guilty about not reciprocating adequately, you can compensate by giving a really nice return present, something a child would treasure. I gave personalized gifts in this princess-and-tiara theme party for Samaira, just the day before Kiaan was born. It was her fifth birthday and I wanted her to feel special, especially because a sibling was on the way. To be honest, I love organizing birthday parties because it is my big moment for my children, so I have had both lavish parties and intimate ones.

I like to have a photographer and a videographer present at these parties, because kids love watching themselves later. It becomes a little album of memories and kids love flipping through it. Years later, it revives their memories. I have a family photographer who maintains our privacy and doesn't give out the photos to anyone. He also knows the moments I like captured, and does not make all of us pose for the camera.

It is important for parents to draw a line somewhere, so that they don't raise spoilt children. If a child wants a party at a fancy hotel poolside, it's fine as long as it fits your budget but then let him invite a finite number of friends, say five to seven close friends. If he's calling more people, then don't buy an extra present for him. You need to deny him something for him to understand the value and importance of the things that you are giving. If you keep making the parties and presents bigger each year, by the time he is 15, he will not care what you give him unless it's a Porsche!

Wingding Wonders: Planning Your Kids Birthday Party

- **Cash Flash:** Keep in mind a budget for your party. Don't go overboard. Discuss what the child wants and who he wants to call and what he would like to eat. If it's going over your budget, you can give alternative solutions to the child to pick from. Either reduce the number of children or find another venue.

- **Bag Binge:** You don't need to blow your budget on goody bags for the kids. You can pick something fun as well as useful, like school bags, pencil boxes, tiffins, water bottles, an assortment of chocolates, books, a small toy, colour pencils, action figurines, puzzles and so on. Mix a few things up and pack them nicely. You can even get the store to make packs. Children love finding many different things in a goody bag.

- **Game Gaga:** Kids need to have something to do at parties. Keeping them occupied with games is important. You'll have about twenty to thirty children high on sugar and extremely active. You need to keep them busy till they get tired. Whether you get a magician, a puppeteer, a tattoo artist, a DJ or a party MC, make sure they know how to keep the kids entertained for as long as it takes!

- **Picture Perfect:** Make sure you have a photographer or a family member who will click a few photos for you. You will be running around welcoming children, getting the cake out, wiping away tears and organizing the entire event. You will not have time to take photos and will later regret not having any moments captured for posterity.

- **Check List:** Book a venue. Send out invites. Pack goody bags. Call the caterer. Buy the birthday child a special outfit. Organize the music. Finalize the decorations. Plan age-appropriate activities. Create a special area for parents who want to sit and chat.

Make sure that you have the party at a time that is convenient for most people who you want should attend. Between 4 and 8 p.m. on a Friday or Saturday is ideal as parents can attend as well and take it easy as there's no school the next day. If your child's birthday falls on a weekday, you can have a small family cake-cutting on that day and a larger party over the weekend. That way you can also split the time and effort. A larger party means that you need to give the kids and adults equal attention, and that can be rather tiring. Two smaller parties allow you to give attention to everyone and make them feel important while your child gets two celebrations and she would obviously love that!

Children want different things at different ages. So, as they grow, you will need to think of different games and other party activities. Younger children would love to play pass-the-parcel and musical chairs. Older children might enjoy races and perhaps a tug-o'-war! You need to make sure that the activities you plan are age appropriate for the invitees. If you have children from different age groups coming over, do something that kids of all ages will love. A friend of mine hosted her son's birthday party at California Pizza Kitchen and she got all the children individual aprons with their names emblazoned on them. All of them had to make their own pizzas and eat them once they were out of the oven. The kids loved this hands-on activity. Another friend had a sleepover as a birthday party for her daughter. So five girls spent the night with the birthday girl and had a blast. Of course, the mothers were informed and a strict watch was kept over the kids. My friend got them new pyjamas and told them ghost stories and everyone had a great time playing and laughing till they all fell asleep, exhausted.

Usually, in public spaces and eateries, there are designated areas for children's birthday parties so that other customers don't get disturbed. Think about it, especially when you plan to take your children out to a restaurant. I think that 3 years is the right age to take a child to a restaurant because before that they just want to move around all over the place and it becomes very difficult to manage them. In fact, till the age of 1, too, it is fine because you can strap them into a high chair but between the time they start crawling and toddling, it becomes a bit of a nightmare.

If the child is old enough to understand, explain to him that you all are going to a restaurant and he has to sit in his place nicely, wait for his food to come and eat it properly. Impress upon him that it is a special occasion that you are going out and he cannot be running around and making a ruckus.

If you can and want to, get a babysitter or a family member to look after your children when you go out for dinner. That way, you can enjoy a nice, quiet meal without the kids. If you must take them, however, do follow these rules:

Bib Cribs: Restaurant Etiquette for Kids and Parents

- **Quarter Plate:** I would not recommend taking children younger than 5 years to fine-dining restaurants and hotels. Other patrons are spending a substantial amount of money to eat there and enjoy themselves and they will not appreciate your children running around! Take your kids to kid-friendly places like McDonald's where they can play with a toy while you have a coffee.

- **Time Tested:** If you have to take the kids out for lunch to a nice place, don't go when it is peak hunger time. Eat early so they get the feel of the new place without disturbing too many other customers.

- **Just Do It:** Always take along something for the child to do while you wait for the food. Colouring pens and a drawing book, jigsaw puzzles or even an iPad that can keep your child occupied will be lifesavers for you.

- **Lite Bite:** For the child, order something that can come quickly and is not too messy. If you order something that is going to take forever to make and may need fancy cutlery to eat, then you're going to have an irate child very soon. Opt for pizzas, pasta, garlic bread, sandwiches and other such things that are easy to manage.

- **Less Mess:** Carry a hand sanitizer along so you don't have to take the child to wash his hands at the beginning of a meal. Also carry wet wipes so that if your child makes a mess, you can wipe his hands and the table or chair or his clothes. Carry paper tissues in case he sneezes and needs to blow his nose—you don't want giant gunk and boogers on the restaurant's napkin!

- **Tot at Work:** If your child gets hyper and wants to run around and scream, well, you can pack your food and leave. You have to be considerate to other customers who haven't paid to be in a playground. You can still eat the yummy food at home but shouldn't let your child run around and behave badly. Tell him that if he behaves badly, he will not be taken out again. And stick to your word.

Trouble is, most people think that since they're paying for being in the restaurant, their child can do whatever he wants. They think, 'Oh, we can give a big tip to the waiter so it's okay!' Even in other public spaces like airplanes and trains and malls, parents think they can just let their kids roam wild and free without caring for other people around. I say no! Disciplining is vital, especially with Indian kids.

Train your child to eat for a full 20 minutes at a dining table at home so that when you take him out, he is used to sitting in one place for some time. Teach him to eat with his mouth closed, not to throw food at other people and not to spill stuff and make a complete mess. Teach him not to spit out the food if he doesn't like it and to always place a napkin on his lap or shirtfront. Start by doing it at home so he'll be used to doing it in restaurants as well. Remind him to say 'please' and 'thank you' to the help at home so he will automatically say it to the waiters in a restaurant.

The most important tip is to lead by example. Don't treat the service industry like a bunch of slaves. Even though they are being paid and you're paying for the service, they're humans who need basic courtesy. Teach your children by extending that courtesy yourself.

Affirmation

A kid's birthday is meant to be fun for everyone.
If it's not fun, I won't do it.
I will teach my kids manners.
They need to be respectful and obedient.
I will enjoy dining out with them when they
are ready, not when I think they are ready.

Walk the Talk: Chatting with Kids about Vital Issues

Age of Rage: Temper Tantrums

What's the best way to handle tantrums? Ignore them! I think kids get brattier when they see their parents getting agitated and reacting to them. So the best thing is to be as calm and composed as possible, try and calm your child down and talk to them. In my home, the naughty-corner concept really helps. If they're naughty, they're sent to sit in a corner with no toys to play with and no one to talk to. Then they have to come back to me and tell me how they think they've changed

and won't do it again. I think discipline is very important. If, however, they are being good and want to play a little longer because they are really enjoying themselves, give them that 10-minute grace. They should also feel that they are getting special treatment. Being your child's friend is very important but there should be a balance between pampering and disciplining, and the children should understand it. They cannot cross boundaries. Yes, they can throw a tantrum, they can get upset, but they should know that they cannot cross a certain boundary. I take my children to Hamleys once a month, sometimes twice, or perhaps to a different toy store like the local one down the road. My rule is that they can pick one thing. Even if we go to a bookstore, they can pick up one or two books at most. They must value what they get.

Normal Abnormal: Handling Disorders and Conditions

Many mothers have kids with attention deficit disorder, obsessive–compulsive disorders, and other such conditions that are not really disabilities. Some kids suffer from post-traumatic stress disorder if something tragic has happened. Certain kids are born with certain disorders. I know it must be painful and very, very tough and it is unimaginable what you may be going through as a mom but we have to be strong for our children because eventually our children depend on us. We have to be strong to make our children strong. All I can say is get family support and perhaps some counselling, just to get over the stress you may be going through as a parent. Do the best you can. Try and be as normal as possible. Talk to your child as a normal human being and treat him with extra love.

Sibling Saga: From Rivalry to Revelry

We need to explain to our children that they are siblings and that they must love each other because they are family. We must also inculcate in them the very important concept of 'sharing is caring'. They have to learn to listen to each other. You have to explain it to them, and make them accept the importance of sisterhood, brotherhood and family over time. You must teach them how to value each other and how to empathize with each other. In my home, if the fighting gets bad, then we call a timeout, in which both of them have to think about what they did wrong and then apologize to each other. They sit in naughty corners and take a few minutes off and then they have to come and say sorry to each other, hug each other and get back to playing. I never shout at my kids. I have noticed that when you shout at kids it just goes in through one ear and is out of the other. You can adopt a sterner tone, most definitely, but never shout or scream at kids—it never works.

Babe's Anatomy: The Growing Body

I think it is very important to have an open chat with your child at all ages about certain issues. You must tell your children what a good touch is and what a bad touch is, right from a young age so they know. I think undressing in front of strangers should not be allowed and not be taught. My daughter is 7 and my son 2; both know about touch and who is allowed to touch them and who is not. By the time she turns 9 or 10, I think I will have a frank discussion with Samaira about bras, menstruation and boys. I'd rather she hears it from me than get some false and misinterpreted information from her peers. That inevitable moment of her period will happen and she will freak out, no matter what. I will not keep a sanitary napkin in her bag because children like to look into each other's bags and they might make fun of her but I will advise her to go to her school doctor or teacher or talk to her nanny, if she is somewhere else besides school. We will also have a chat about bras and undergarments but I'll wait till she's 10. I'll start her with a training/sports bra and then move to sizes. I will want to take her shopping rather than her going with friends and picking out the wrong things.

The Social Network: Phones, Emails, Chats

With older kids, mothers should monitor their Facebook sessions and other chats and generally keep track of what they are doing on the computer all the time. If you give your kids a BlackBerry phone, you should know who they are sending out Messenger requests to or adding to their contacts. My daughter and son both have phones but they are for their respective nannies to call me. They have different activities and routines so they might be in two different places while I'm on a set or in a meeting so the two phones are given to the maids, who use them only to communicate with me. I am very particular that even the driver is not allowed to touch those phones, even if it is left in the car and is ringing. Also, don't let your child ever get to a phase where he refuses to share his phone or laptop, saying, 'No! This is mine and you can't see it.' Parents should have access to everything and should monitor the time the kids spend on gizmos as well as the sites they visit when surfing the net. You should decide the sites and things they are allowed to see, and put a block on the other things that they are not to see because there is so much out there which their young minds cannot comprehend yet.

Heart-Throbs: Crushes and Heartbreaks

Older children will start having crushes and talking about boyfriends and girlfriends. It is important for parents to keep an open mind and talk to their children about what they're feeling. It could be quite innocent. Make sure you allow the boy or girl in question to come home and talk to you. Interact with your child and their crush. Talk to that child's parents as well to keep a lookout. Never allow them to stay in a closed room together. This is the time to be your child's friend. If they're open with you, they will take your advice. If you advise too much, they will shut you out. Listen as much as you can. If they have a case of heartbreak, take them out for some shopping or ice cream and listen to them. They need to know you are there for them. But remember to set boundaries. They should not be allowed to go partying by themselves or come home late or stay alone at any place. Be careful till they finally grow up!

Tough Tots: School Bullies and Bad Words

If your kid is small, you must tell his teacher if certain children in his group/class pull his hair or tease him or push him around, whatever the case. It is important for you to tell your child that if anybody harms him, he must come and tell you or tell his teacher about it and not stay quiet about it. You should encourage your child to come and speak to you about everything. Also tell him not to tolerate any insult, ever. If anybody behaves badly with him, he should not accept it because if somebody is being naughty or rude, he must tell the person not to be rude. If you see children hitting each other—and when kids are 2 years or 2½ years old, they will—just explain to them that hitting is not good. You also have to tell them not to use bad language. In my house, even a 'shut up' is reacted to with a 'hawwww', meaning that it is not a nice thing to say. Kiaan understands that. It is good to start teaching children these things when they are young.

Material Girl: Comparing and Envying

I always tell Samaira to be happy with what she has. I say, 'You should be happy with what your family can afford, and you should not compare yourself with others.' Ever since she's turned 6–7 years old, she says things like: 'Oh Mama, this girl got this fairy bag' or 'My friend got this doll from America' . . . So my response is: 'Well, if you can't go there or you haven't been there, you can still admire that doll!' You have to start explaining that to them because otherwise there is no end to keeping up and your child will get thoroughly spoilt and won't learn any values. One of her friends lives in a bungalow so she wants to know why we don't have a bungalow and I tell her that this is our house and she has her room, her space, which she should be happy with. This is what her parents can afford to give her, so she should be happy with it and proud of it, of whatever she has. If you start teaching them all of this at a young age, then material things will not affect them later.

Squeaky Clean: Hygiene Check

My mother used to play a game with Kareena and I when we were young. She would wait outside the bathroom and say, 'Let me see how many minutes who takes to scrub themselves really well!' So there used to be a competition of cleaning and bathing and then she would make us stand and check our ears, check our teeth, check our arms and give us 10 on 10 or 9 on 10 and so on. I do the same thing with my children now. Though Kiaan is young and needs to be bathed, I make sure I time my older one and give her points and I give points to Kiaan for looking so clean. There is so much dust these days, and it plays a very big role in kids falling ill, getting allergies, catching colds and coughs . . . Dust gathers in soft stuffed toys in the kids' room, in the rugs and carpets and so on. Clean all of these regularly. It's best to avoid them if possible.

This friend of mine would tell her daughter, 'Pick up your toys and keep them in your cupboard.' The daughter would say, 'That's your job!' We have to teach kids from a young age to keep their toys away after play. I know that kids of 2 or 3 years of age are not going to do that, but it is good to encourage them. Keeping a child's room clean is very important. Clean their bathrooms and floors with antiseptics like Dettol; that is what I do because they drop things on and pick things off the floor and kids are coming over constantly with shoes and muck and crumbs all over. Keep the room as sanitized as you can.

Top Three Values to Give Your Kids

1. Respect for self
2. Respect for money
3. Respect for family

I think these three things are very, very important: to know and appreciate your own self-worth, to value money and understand that you have to work hard for it, and to love and respect your family, always aware that you need to work on it to make it work. If you give your kids these three values, you have done a great job and raised a good human being!

The Most Important Lesson to Teach Your Child

Your kids must be taught to never talk to strangers. Teach them to shout for help if a stranger tries to coax them away from their place of safety or from a maid or family member. Tell your children that if a person speaks to them about their private parts or touches them inappropriately, they must immediately scream for help and report it to someone they trust. Even if such an incident has happened already, tell them that they should not feel ashamed to tell their mommy or daddy.

Affirmation
I will tackle all problems with a calm head.
I will raise good kids and give them positive energy.

I, Me, Myself: It's Me Time!

If I had one whole day off from being a mother, I would definitely go in for a spa treatment. After that, I would have a leisurely lunch with some friends and come home and watch endless hours of TV. But then again, honestly speaking, I would not want a day off. I love being a mother and I love being around my children.

I think now I don't even have the time or the patience to do my nails or get a blow-dry! It's as if these things have become chores that I would like to rush through, all the while thinking, 'Oh my God! Do I really need to do this?' You know, when you have kids, you are constantly thinking about them and their plans and their homework and what is happening with them and what needs to be bought for them. We moms tend to neglect ourselves but we should take that one day off or perhaps 2–3 hours of me time for ourselves once a week. It is important to rejuvenate for the coming week. Try it—get a manicure or pedicure, get a nice head massage or hair spa or some threading and waxing or whatever girly thing you want to do for yourself because it is vital to relax.

Whether you choose to take a day off in a week or a few hours every day or even a few hours once a week, make sure you have a good support system looking after your children while you are under the radar. It is extremely important for you to go and do your own thing and connect with your friends or get a massage occasionally. You become a better mother by pampering your body and mind. Your positive energy radiates from you on to your kids. When mom's happy, they are happy too.

Remember to send your children away before you start pampering yourself or find ways to relax. Having screaming children in the house or clingy kids demanding your attention will not help you de-stress!

Downtime Diva: How to Let Go and Just Relax

• **Bubble Binge:** If you have a bathtub, take a long and luxurious bath while the children are away on a play date. Throw in some lavender or camomile bath salts, froth up some bubbles just for yourself this time and relax for 30 minutes. After that, have a nice cup of hot tea or a cold lemon soda and sleep for a while.

• **What You Knead:** Go to a spa and get a long, relaxing massage. Or call the local *maalishwali* at home to relax your muscles. Light some aromatic candles in the room and make your own spa.

• **Book Nook:** Getting lost in a different world rekindles your imagination. If you've been only doing mommy things and reading fairy tales to your kids, now read books that you like. If you can't handle a serious read, pick up some light chick lit that you can skim through and enjoy.

• **Buddy Bonding:** Connect with your friends. Having an adult conversation with adults is a great way to rejuvenate your mind. Meet a few single gal pals and listen to their stories and laugh out loud. Share experiences with some mothers or just-married friends so you can give advice, remember your old days and be around people who you identify with. Continuously talking to your husband or family about your children can get tiresome.

• **Flick Trick:** The latest blockbuster or a new art-house film has been released and you've been dying to go watch it. But since it's not animated, you can't take your kids. Here's your chance to go watch a film alone. No crying, no bathroom breaks, no ice cream demands! You can sit quietly with your cup of coffee and enjoy the film by yourself. You don't even need to find friends to go with—just take that time out for yourself and enjoy the experience.

• **Rhythm and No Blues:** Listening to good music really elevates your soul. If it's foot-tapping, get up and dance all by yourself. It burns calories and it is fun.

• **Wonder Walk:** Some fresh outdoor air and a brisk walk around the park will get your heart racing and be good for your mind as well. If you have a pet, it will be good if you take it for a walk instead of sending it off with a servant. This way it gets to bond with you as well instead of feeling left out with the arrival of the kids.

• **Salon Stint:** A nice body treatment can lift your spirits tremendously. Looking good makes you feel good. Be sure to go on a dinner date later with hubby or meet some friends to show off your glam look.

• **Hobby Redux:** If you love knitting, sewing, playing a sport, painting, writing, or some such thing, take out a few hours in a week to do this. Don't give up. Join a club or a group that can keep you motivated.

• **Sexual Healing:** Connecting with your partner even after you become a mother is extremely important. He must never feel left out. Sex is also good for the skin as it releases all the toxins from the body. It is a good cardiovascular workout! It also gives you an emotional boost and lets you sleep better. You feel like a woman, not just a mother.

Before you became a mother, you were an independent woman. You studied, you worked, you partied, you relaxed. Just because you've become a mother doesn't mean you need to give up all those things that defined you. Yes, the definition will alter slightly because you have one more thing to manage, and that will take up a lot of your time. But managing time and finding a balance is the key to a successful life. If you consider motherhood to be the most serious job you'll ever do, make it as high a priority as letting it take up 50 per cent of your life. The remainder needs to still be cut up into different sections: 25 per cent needs to go into your work or any activity that keeps you occupied, 15 per cent needs to go into the rest of your family (parents, siblings, cousins, family functions) and 10 per cent needs to go into pampering yourself. Of course, your spouse must remain high on your agenda and you must give him time over and above all this so he doesn't feel neglected and your marriage doesn't suffer. But I would not recommend that you make motherhood a 100 per cent of your life. Whatever activity you choose to do in your downtime, make sure you do it without your children and that there's much happiness while you're doing it. No guilt, no regrets. Rekindle the real you. Look at yourself in the mirror and ask, 'Who am I? What do I want from life? Am I happy? How can I be happier?' You will find the answers within you if you take the time to ask these questions in a silent space when you're by yourself. Do this regularly every time you feel upset.

Mothers feel frustrated on a daily basis. I know I do. It's natural. We all love being moms but we're also tired with the same routines and the same tantrums. And yet, the little moments that give us joy outnumber the ones that frustrate us. If we had to be moms all over again, we'd do it in a heartbeat. We want to be needed. We like being depended on. We like the fact that our children are helpless without us. It gives us great power. Even though we are raising strong and independent individuals, somewhere deep in our hearts we want to know that they can't really function 100 per cent without us. Perhaps just 90 per cent!

After Samaira, I didn't work for many years. After Kiaan, I decided to go out and do a movie. It took me many years to realize that I need to love myself as well. All my love can't be given away to my two kids. I need to value what I do and who I am, for only then will my children value me. Learning to focus on the positive will make you a good mom, and it will only come if you give yourself time. I firmly believe that you need at least half an hour to yourself every day, and a few hours to yourself every week.

After I pack my kids off to school, I do my yoga with a home instructor. For that 1 hour, I devote all my energy to my body and my breathing. By the end, I feel so good that I don't care what else happens in the day. Once in a while, I go out for a coffee and eat a chocolate pastry to indulge. I even go shopping for myself. A little retail therapy always cheers me up.

Whether you're a working mother or a stay-at-home mom, you can always take out time to relax. It's all about managing your time.

Clockwork Mom: How to Manage Your Time

• **Plan Weekly Menus:** If you buy your groceries once a week and stock your fridge, plan a menu for the week for your cook or yourself with healthy snacks as well as mini indulgences. That done, you are pretty much sorted. Planning what your family eats can be more time-consuming than you might imagine. If your children and staff have a meal plan to follow through the day, then even if you're out or at work, they won't fuss too much and you won't be stressed whether they are eating correctly.

• **Structure Your Day:** Make lists of what is (1) top priority, (2) can be done later, and (3) can be postponed. For instance, stay-at-home moms need to get a leaking faucet fixed as priority 1. Bathing the baby can be postponed by a few hours if there are too many things to do. And dropping clothes off at the dry-cleaner's can be postponed till when you're ready. Working mothers can do the same with their work.

• **Delegate Chores:** You can't do everything by yourself. You need help. Everyone agrees you're superwoman, so now give yourself a break. Hire a nanny, cook, driver, etc. Get a family member to help, join a support group, find other mothers and babysitters. There are plenty of ways to make your life a little easier. It might mean spending a little extra money but it will give you tremendous peace. Your peace of mind is more important than those extra hundreds of rupees that you will shell out. It will keep you positive and make your child a better person as well.

• **Say No:** Refuse to attend parties, family functions, lunches, dinners, extra meetings and so on if you're already stressed. If someone's cousin's cousin is getting married and they've sent you a card, you don't have to attend. They'll understand that you're trying to manage a child and work. You don't owe anyone anything. Send a gift later if they're close to you.

• **Prep Your Car:** Keep an extra set of essentials in your car. Keep handy health bars for children, packets of biscuits, bananas and other food items that don't perish quickly. Don't keep water bottles though, as water must be fresh. Keep a bag with the baby's clothes, diapers, bibs and bottles or, if you have a toddler, an extra set of clothes, shoes, wet wipes, a packet of biscuits, books, colouring paper and pencils. Also keep an umbrella. Keep a set of formal clothes for yourself as well. If your kids are in the car or you're going to work but have forgotten something in the morning in the mad rush, you have an extra supply and are not worried about returning home to collect it. Make sure you replenish the items used in the evening when you get home.

• **Bathe at Night:** If your child wakes up late and takes for ever to get ready for school, bathe him at night. In the morning, brush his teeth, wash his face, dab on some powder, get him into clean clothes and send him to school. This way, he takes a bath at the end of the day when he's sweaty and grimy from playing all day and you save some time in the morning from this chore. Children older than 3 should bathe twice a day. Moisturize with a soft baby lotion so his skin doesn't become dry, or use powder if it's extremely hot.

• **Switch Off Electronics:** All through the day, you get emails, chats, pings, Tweets, Facebook updates and so on. You need to switch your phone to silent mode while you get ready and get your child ready. If you start answering everything in the morning, your stress level will rise and you will definitely forget something. Keep it silent till you've got a little free time.

• **Make It Fun:** Put on your favourite music while waking up. Get your child to groove to a familiar beat when she's getting ready. Currently, Samaira is listening to songs from the film *Cocktail* and loves to get up and dance a bit before she has her glass of milk. I give her those extra 5 minutes so she's happy doing what she wants to.

• **Leave the Mess:** By hanging all the towels, putting the clothes back in the cupboard, aligning shoes and rearranging books, you're not doing yourself a favour. If your house looks like a mess in the morning, let it be. You're not having visitors drop in and assess you for tidiness. You have a job to do. So focus on that. Clear the mess later.

• **Work the Internet:** Pay your bills online. Figure out if there are any services that can deliver things or pick up items. Try to do as much shopping as you can online. Keep the rest of the chores for the weekend. Bank work and doctor's appointments that need to be attended to personally can be done on a Saturday while someone else is looking after your children.

Meditation also releases stress and centres you. Switch off all phones, lock your door and sit in meditation for 10 minutes a day and gradually increase it to 30 minutes. Let there be complete silence. Let thoughts enter your head and then remove the thoughts. Meditation gives you incredible peace and helps you deal with the stress of daily life better.

In the morning, when I wake up, I have two glasses of hot water. Every day, I take primrose oil tablets, cod liver oil tablets and flaxseeds. You can grind flaxseeds and sprinkle the powder over your cereal. These are little clever things that are nice for your body. Many women like to drink fresh juices, which I don't, but fresh vegetable juice is also very good for your skin. Drink it within 2 minutes of making it to get the best effect.

I have a friend who left her 1½-year-old child and went off to the US with her husband for a vacation. I have another friend who left both her children with her husband and went off on a 3-week holiday with her gal pals. I think a vacation is a must for every woman, but it depends on the mother. Don't go if you're going to be crying away, wanting to be back with your child. If you do go, I would advise that you go during school vacation so you're not stressed about who's taking them to school and what's happening with their lives. Leave your kids in good care with parents and nannies and check in on them every day. When you choose to take that trip, don't feel guilty. You deserve a little rest and relaxation. It doesn't take away from you being a mother—and you come back rejuvenated, to look after your children with a fresh mind and a positive outlook.

Three Tips on How Not to Lose Your Identity

1.   Always be yourself, whatever your personality is.

2.   Don't try to compete with a new mom or with your friends.

3.   Don't obsess about going back to being the person you were, and don't obsess over motherhood either. Strike the right balance.

Affirmation

I deserve some time for myself.

It makes me a better mother.

Enfant Encore: Planning Your Next Baby

It is a matter of choice, but I feel that the ideal time to start planning your next baby is once your child is a year and a half old. Then your children can grow up together, more or less. It's very helpful because they can do a lot of things together, like going to school or other activity classes or picnics with friends. It also helps them bond very well. Also, they say that your body takes a year to go back to its original size after a baby, so then again a year and a half is a good interval after which you can start planning. Another way of looking at it is that you can plan the next baby as soon as your child is slightly independent. For the mom who has babies within 2 years, the first 6 months will be really harrowing but, beyond that, I think it will be a blessing. It is better to finish up with the diaper phase of your life than getting into it much later and thinking, 'Oh my God! I have forgotten everything!' When you've just had a baby 2 years ago, you know you're still in the mommy zone and the diaper zone and sterilizing-bottles zone—it is easier to know what to do with your kids.

I had Kiaan when Samaira was already 5, so I had to learn the whole process all over again. Of course, I did remember most of it but all that sterilizing bottles and changing nappies and feeding at midnight left me quite exhausted. I was also older and it took time to get the hang of things. It was more difficult to lose weight and get into shape since I was into my thirties and my metabolism had slowed down. If you're a young mother, having two kids close to each other will allow you to bounce back quicker so don't wait till you're on the other side of 30 to have the second one.

I, personally, feel that every woman should have two children. The bond that Kareena and I share is something I will cherish forever. I don't know what kind of person I would have been if I didn't have a younger sister looking out for me or someone I could look out for. Even though we are close to our parents, the connection that we have between just the two of us is something that we can never share with our mom or dad or anyone else.

I also feel, quite honestly, that you don't need a horde of kids for them to bond. More than two kids and you're adding to the population and burdening yourself financially, emotionally, physically. You're also putting a strain on your marriage since you'll want to look after your children, your career, your house and may not be able to devote as much time as your partner needs and wants. So before you go in for a third or fourth child, please think of all these things and then take a call. Of course, at the end of the day, it is your body and your choice, and each child is a blessing for every family.

Before going in for the next child, make sure you get all your and your partner's tests done again and are given a clean bill of health. Take your medicines and start planning gradually. The process is the same as having the first child but this time you are older and wiser. You also have to take care of the first child so you need to take all the precautions of looking after yourself and staying fit. Once you're pregnant, you will not be able to pick up your older one very often so you should be particular about spending time with her and talking to her about the younger sibling, making her look forward to the baby so that she won't feel jealous later.

Baby Boom: Tips for Planning Your Second Kid

- **Mind the Gap:** I would recommend keeping a gap of at least a year or two between two children. You need time to get back into shape and into a pattern of resting and sleeping. You need to wean off your first child. Let your body heal before you give your kid a sibling.

- **Lean on Them:** You'll need a solid support system before you have your second child. Make sure you have a nanny or a family member who can help with the older child while you look after the newborn.

- **Pass the Test:** Get all your tests done so you know that everything is okay with you. If you're on any post-partum depression medicines, consult your doctor on how to handle the pregnancy.

- **Take Your Time:** You might feel that a certain time is just right to have the second baby but putting pressure on your husband and yourself is not going to help. Take your time in conceiving and if it does not happen within a certain period, ask your doc for alternatives.

- **Counsel the Older Child:** You must prepare your older child about what will happen once the newborn comes and what his role will be. You need to spend as much time as you can with him and make sure he doesn't feel left out. You should also guide him to help you while you're pregnant. He can keep his room clean so you don't have to bend so much. He can fetch his own things instead of making you get up all the time. Sit with him to pore over photograph albums of his baby days. Point out the different stages of rolling, crawling, walking. Let him know that the baby will also go through all of that, and grow big enough to play with him one day. Look at recent photos of him and point out all the things that he can do now like run and jump and swing and paint. Tell him about all the things that make him wonderful. A special gift 'from the baby' to him may help him feel positive about this new little stranger in his house.

- **Clean All Clothes:** Make sure that all the clothes you plan to pass on to the second kid are cleaned, ironed and in good condition. You still need to get new diapers, feeding bottles and nipples and a whole range of new baby things if your first child has used his extensively. You can't pass on any germs to your newborn!

- **Make Some Space:** Perhaps your first child is still sleeping in your room. Perhaps the entire family shares one sleeping area. You will need to figure out where the older child sleeps later so his routine is not jeopardized because of a crying newborn at night.

- **Manage Your Finances:** Make sure that you have enough finances, or take a bank loan if you need to be financially sound. A second baby does have its own expenses and it's not as if you can pass on everything from the first to the second. You will need more baby stuff and the pregnancy and delivery will cost you a bit. Be alert about your household expenditure and curb your luxury buying if you need to.

- **Plan the Method:** If you've had your first child by caesarean section, you might need to wait for 2 years before you can conceive again and hope to have the second one by natural delivery. Check with your doctor and take all precautions, else you may have another caesarean.

- **Take Enough Rest:** This is not your first pregnancy but don't think that you need any less rest. Your body still needs plenty of sleep. You need to put up your feet as much as you can, whenever and wherever you can. After the birth, don't feel compelled to spend all your time with your first child when the second one is sleeping. You need time to rest as well since you will be feeding and your body has just gone through labour or surgery. Don't be too hard on yourself. Children understand. Your health is most important. You don't want a situation where you are unfit and cannot look after any of your children.

Mothers need to de-stress before they have a second kid. Ideally, if you potty-train your first child, then you don't have to worry about cleaning the first kid's diapers before you start changing a newborn's! Stock up on healthy food and start reducing the junk you eat. Folic acid, calcium, proteins, omega 3 and vitamin C need to be taken on a daily basis all over again. Do not neglect your body just because you think you've been there, done that. Every pregnancy is different. If you didn't have morning sickness earlier, you might develop symptoms now. If you didn't gain any weight then but feel you've already bloated up, you must start taking precautions. Your pregnancy is different just as your labour will be different. You are bringing another human being into the world. It's all different! You need to read the beginning of this book all over again and do it correctly once more.

Affirmation

I'm excited about having a sibling for my child.
I shall be healthy for my kids and positive
about any new thing that happens to me.

Tot Spirit, Teen Spirit: Tackling Toddlers and Teenagers

If there's one thing I'm thankful for, it is that I have decent children who don't break things in other people's homes. I have seen kids who run around like mad and knock over tables and pick up vases and slam them on to the floor! And their moms will turn around and say, *'Arey woh to bachcha hi hai!'* ('He's just a child!') And I want to scream, 'Yes, he's a child, but you're the responsible adult who should tell him what to do and what not to do!' I can't stand people who think that kids should be allowed to run amok in other people's homes and public places. If your child breaks anything or spoils the upholstery at your friend's place, at least offer to pay for the damage. If she doesn't need the money, send her a lovely bouquet of flowers or buy her a very nice present so she appreciates your gesture. And don't take your child to their house the next time. Invite them out to a kid-friendly place or take the other mom out separately for a relaxing coffee or to a local club. Meanwhile, teach your child that it's not right to be destructive.

Hypodermic Horrors: Getting Kids Vaccinated

You must get your children vaccinated. I know there are many tales about some drugs but I don't believe them. If there is a drug out there that can prevent chickenpox and polio and immunize my child so that he can have a healthy life, I will give it to him. I am not going to wait for medical science to find a better drug. What's the harm? If your child has the opportunity to lead a healthy, fruitful life with a sound mind and a good body, you would not want to deprive him of that because of something someone said. Check with your doctor what the available and indispensable vaccines are. I gave even the optional ones to my children. I never want to take a chance with so many diseases spreading around. There are some that need to be given at birth and then at regular intervals, with boosters after a few years. Keep a tab on their immunization charts.

Peepers and Pearlies: Checking Eyes and Teeth

Around 4 years is a good age to get your child's eyes and teeth examined medically. Many parents do not tend to check the kids' eyes because they think that the kids can see just fine but kids may not realize that there is a problem in their vision and will try to adapt to the disorder, if there is one. So, it is very important to get their eyes checked. Also, you need to get their teeth checked every 6 months. You should brush the kids' teeth as early as when they are a few months old. Get a soft-bristle brush that you can slip on to your finger and massage their gums, teeth and tongue with. Get them into the habit well before their first birthday and continue doing it twice a day till they can brush on their own. Let them pick out their own toothbrush and flavoured toothpaste so that they feel it's a fun thing to do.

The Mane Thing: Going for Haircuts

I did not have a *mundan* ceremony for either of my kids. I feel that hair growth is genetic and no amount of mundan can improve your child's hair growth or texture. Samaira had her first haircut in London when she was a little over a year. I took a picture and got it framed, a photo of her sitting on the chair with a little bit of her baby locks! Kiaan's first haircut was when he was 7 months old because he had lovely curly little locks that had begun to come on to his eyes and had to be trimmed. Now, I have a guy who comes home to cut Kiaan's hair, while Samaira goes to the local salon for a very simple, very basic trim. You must keep your child's hair away from his eyes. Also, trim it regularly and wash it at least twice a week with baby/kids' shampoo.

Lock, Stock and Barrel: Travelling with Kids

If you can, take a maid along on long trips so you can have some undisturbed time with your husband or relatives or yourself. If you have to cater to your children all by yourself, it gets tough to do anything together as a couple. I know people hire babysitters from the hotels they stay in but I'm very conservative so I wouldn't do it. Also, I think it's nice to take your maid so she gets to see a new place too and can look after the children while you do something on your own for some time. I have also travelled without maids and it's been a wonderful vacation for the kids. I enjoyed myself, though I couldn't do *all* the things I wanted to.

Money Money Money: Giving Pocket Allowance

The best way to teach children the value of money is to start giving them a weekly allowance. The best time to start is around 7–8 years when the child has understood basic mathematics. Check with other mums how much they give. You can give a basic allowance so that the child can buy what he wants, and you can add to it if it's a special occasion. For his birthday week, for instance, you can give double the amount. Tell the child that if he wants anything, other than what you send in his tiffin for instance, he must use his allowance. You can also tell him to save enough to buy birthday gifts for his friends or family members. Of course, you can supplement it whenever you feel the amount is too little for a decent present but the child will learn the value of money this way. Don't give out more money whenever he runs out. If he's spent it all by Wednesday, don't replenish it. Let him wait till Sunday or whichever day you dole out the money. Don't give extra money if he does well in class—he should do so in any case. But give him a bonus if he does any extra bit of work in the house that he doesn't do regularly, say he helps you clean the bookrack or does his own laundry!

Parental Guidance: Blocking Sites and Channels

As your child grows older, he'll go from playing with toys to playing on the PSP to googling on the Internet. Sometimes, I think that when Bebo and I were young and didn't have anything but a bat and a ball and a few dolls, it was so much easier for parents. Nowadays, we have to be very careful what we let our children watch or surf or hear. There is enough pornography out there, and too many online predators and cyber bullies that can lure your child. Not only do you need to block certain sites, but you also need to get net savvy and check their online history. As for TV, don't watch any adult programmes in front of the children as they get influenced and might start repeating things they hear and see. Age-appropriate TV shows are very important.

You must educate the kids about the dangers of the Net. You must also keep an open mind and if they stumble upon something and start asking questions, always answer as truthfully and as age appropriately as you can. Don't hide anything from your children. Become a friend from the beginning so that they can confide in you. When you need to be strict, take on the parent role and tell them that they just cannot be allowed to chat with strangers. Also, let them use the computer or laptop or iPad only when you're around or somewhere where you can see what they're doing. As soon as they start to get secretive, start talking to them more about their friends and whose status they've liked on Facebook and so on. Open discussions help. Staying alert really helps.

And if you're completely scared that your 13-year-old is going astray, you can block websites on your home computer without investing in expensive software. Here's the trick for Windows PCs: click the 'Start' button and select 'Run'. Type in *notepad c:\WINDOWS\system32\drivers\etc\hosts* in the Run box that appears. You will see a new Notepad window on your screen with some cryptic info. Don't panic. Just go to the last line of the file, hit 'Enter' and type in the following:

127.0.0.1 orkut.com

127.0.0.1 facebook.com

127.0.0.1 myspace.com

Save the file and exit. That's it. None of the above sites will now open on your computer.

Smells Like Teen Spirit: Dating, Etc.

Congratulations! You have a teenager on your hands! A whole new set of problems will arise with this group of people who suddenly think they're no longer your kids but individuals whom you just don't understand. They will have crushes and heartbreaks. They will try to hide many things from you. If you talk to them, they'll slam their room door on your face and tell you to leave them alone. Then you'll hang your head and wonder where your sweet child went and who this monster is, whom you can't get rid of! I have a friend who was on her daughter's BBM. Every time she had a fight with her daughter, she would ping her about how it upset her and ask her what it would take for the daughter to open up to her mother. Another friend 'friended' her son on Facebook to see who his friends were. You have to try everything to get through to your teenage kids. If you bond very well with them, it is likely that when they start having a crush on someone, they will come and tell you. Invite the boy/girl in question over for tea and cakes and get to know him/her a little. They will probably not get married and settle down but at least you are aware of who's who and what's what. Also, do have The Talk of safe sex with your child and tell them that it's not okay to have sex just because others are doing it. If they don't want to talk to you about it, get the help of a cousin or an aunt they're close to so that they can confide in them.

Not Too Haute: Forbidden Fashion

You want your girl to wear a prim and proper salwar-kameez-dupatta when she goes out but she wants to wear the tiniest skirt and a crop top that leaves nothing to the imagination. You have a fight. She wears what you tell her to. She storms out. And she changes into what she wants to wear in a hotel restroom. You lose anyway! The solution is to stop being ultra-fashion-conscious yourself. If you pore over fashion magazines and wear short dresses in front of her, she will think it's okay for her too. Remember Newton's third law? For every action, there is an equal and opposite reaction. Understand your teenager—if you set a good example, chances are she will follow it. This is also the time to negotiate, and all your years of bargaining with the Janpath jewellery seller should come to use here. If she wants to wear hot pants, tell her she can wear Bermuda shorts. If she scoffs and says 'skirt', then settle for a long skirt. You will probably come to a mid-point where she can wear a knee-length skirt for now and a lovely top. You can even go shopping with her for a whole new set of clothes and pick the things both of you agree upon! Most importantly, teach your child from a very young age to respect herself, no matter how she looks. Also, do let her have her way sometimes with an added bit of dash. If she wants to get lip gloss or wear black nail polish, you know it's going to go away in a few weeks. So let her feel she's done something different, which you know is not overtly sexual.

My Body, My Canvas: Make-Up, Piercings, Tattoos

I think you should set a time limit for your children to experiment with things they want to do. Tell them they are not allowed to wear proper make-up till they hit 16 or 18 years. Reinforce the fact that they have great skin and people will love them for their natural beauty and it's not good to look older than they are. I think we need to get to the root cause of why they want to do certain things. Most children follow their peers and a few do it because they want to rebel. Talking to them, understanding them and spending time with them will help you as well. And if they simply have to get that tattoo or piercing, make sure it's from a hygienic and safe place, so that there are no complications later. Children need to learn on their own as well and we can't keep holding their hands all through life.

One-Woman Army: Single Moms, Divorced Moms

It is not easy being a single parent. Period. It is double the responsibility for the one parent and it can be very tough on the children. So if you feel that you can make the marriage work, please do so for the sake of the child. Go to a counsellor, try every possible thing you can before you decide to separate or get a divorce.

Having said that, I think it is better for children not to see their parents fighting. If you have reached the end of your tether, take a breather from each other before you get back together. Moreover, if you cannot get back together, remember that a divorce is not the end of the world. You and your child will survive. Remember to get enough support for your family when you make this choice. You will need help in raising your children and if you are going through the trauma as well, it will be difficult for you to explain the situation to them.

The most important thing I want to tell you is this: do not fall apart! It is not easy but you have to accept that it is not going to be easy, and you have to believe that you will get through it and emerge stronger.

The road ahead, going solo, is going to be difficult because you will be alone emotionally and you will need to make decisions for your child on your own. But life is long and time is a great healer and it will get easier.

Frankly, I do not think you need a man's purse to live well. I am a strong believer in the strength of women. We all have it within us to take on whatever there is in this Universe, whatever hand we are dealt. That is my philosophy in life. We must always look at the positive aspect of any situation. If it makes you happy to remarry and you want a different kind of family and if the new man accepts your child, then do it. Do not marry a person only because you think he will make a great dad. Always be around with your child and the new dad until your child is comfortable.

Keep yourself open to a new life, a happier life. Always believe in yourself.

Solo Flights: How to Succeed at Single Parenting

• **Get Reliable Help:** If you are a working woman, make sure you have a good support system for your children to be looked after. Either have a family member come over regularly or hire a good nanny who can manage your child. Your child should also be involved in many activities so he can be busy while you're not around. Put him in a good day care where they will look after him and you won't need to worry. Even if you're a stay-at-home mom, make sure the child is occasionally away from the house in school or play dates so you can get some time for yourself.

• **Spend Quality Time:** Quality matters, not quantity, when it comes to time. Spend enough time with the kid when you're home. Even if you have a few hours with him, make them count. Do not be on the telephone constantly or stuck to the TV. When you come home to your child, pay attention to what he wants to play with, ask relevant questions about his day in school and his extra lessons. Help him change, get him ready for bed and read a book to him or with him. Those few hours with you might mean more to him than two parents who have no time for him.

- **Do Not Overindulge:** Just because you are a single parent, you do not need to make up for the spouse's love by buying your child everything he wants. You will turn him into a brat and he will respect you less if you try to buy his love. Be firm on what you can give and what you do not want to give. Set clear boundaries, timings, structures and routines. Keep to the same schedule and pattern as when you were married. Love them enough to say 'NO'!

- **Meet a Counsellor:** Sometimes, with one parent not around, children feel a huge burden and develop emotional problems. These may manifest as tics, stammers or defects in body language. Immediately go to a counsellor and ask for help. You do not want this to develop into a lifelong situation that you did not catch in time. Do not think it will go away by indulging him. Do not try to get back together with your spouse for the child's sake. It needs to be fixed by a professional. Make an appointment as soon as you detect something awry.

- **Always Be Honest:** With very young kids, you can get by with excuses like their dad is travelling or sleeping in the office that night. Older kids are very intuitive, though, and I think you need to tell them that you're separated and that both of you love him but live separately. Tell teenagers the truth because they can guess and it is very difficult to regain their trust if you lie to them.

I would firmly advise you not to think of a separation/divorce as the worst thing that could have happened to you and your family. India has progressed to a stage where a divorcee status hardly matters. What matters is that you raise a positive, independent, well-behaved and intelligent child. I must mention that my mother made a lot of sacrifices for us when we were growing up. Kareena and I were always her top priority. She raised us to be independent, grounded women with strong values. Whether you choose to do it alone or with your spouse, you both need to be positive about it. Your parenting circumstances are less important than you actually being there for the child.

Lonely Planet Guide: Top Ten Tips for Single Parents

1. **Strike a Balance:** You must realize that you're one person and you're doing the best you can. You can't be at all places at once. You need to prioritize. If your work meeting is more important than taking the child to a birthday party, go for the meeting. Take the child to a special place later. If you can postpone the meeting, take

the child and let him have a good time. Find a balance. Don't think that by working continuously and earning enough to give your child everything he wants, you're doing him a favour. He just needs more time from you, rather than an extra toy.

2.   Stay Positive: If you slump into depression, if you think that it's the end of the world, if you wallow in misery and self-pity, your child is going to pick up your vibes and become a different person. You need to stay positive for the sake of your child. Many families have separated parents and it's no big deal. The children turn out to be great. You just need to be strong and instil the values in your kids as you would for yourself. Think, 'What would my role model do in this situation?' Keep happy quotes all around your room. Write them on Post-its and stick them everywhere, on your refrigerator, on the bathroom mirror. Keep yourself motivated.

3.   Don't Expect: Your partner has moved on or you have decided to leave him. Now don't expect that person to take an interest in your life or help out too much with the child. It's your responsibility. You can't say, 'Come home and spend time with the kid' or 'Don't you think you should be taking him for classes?' The spouse may not care. If he wants to be there, he will be. Until then, you look after your child to the best of your ability.

4.   Don't Bad-Mouth: So you have gone through a bitter break-up and mud-slinging has happened. This does not mean that you should say awful things about your spouse to your child. You don't need to influence your child against the other parent. The marriage broke up because either or both of you fell out of love and were not compatible any more—the child had nothing to do with it. You cannot corrupt an innocent mind. Hold your tongue about your spouse in front of the child or when speaking to someone else with the child around. They are susceptible to tones and words, and will pick up what you say.

5.   Encourage Bonding: Security, safety and mental well-being are of utmost importance for the children. It is hard but, in the long run, having two separate parents who love the child and support each other even if they're not living together makes a huge impact on the child's growth. Let the father take the child to a new 3D movie that you've told the child he can watch on the weekend. Or take him to practise a sport he's been participating in, in his classes. Encourage the bonding between them but don't force too much. If the child just wants to be around you, let the father be around while you sit and read a book so they can eventually spend time together instead of you taking up the activity that the child wants to do. Children need their mothers at all times.

6.   **Do Not Befriend:** Don't suddenly go from parent mode to friend mode with your child. You don't want to confide in your child about the broken marriage and all your marital problems. He is still a child. He cannot take sides and it is unfair to expect him to do so. He cannot look at either of his parents with hatred because of what the other has said or done to them. Confide the feelings against your spouse to a friend, family member or a therapist but never to your child.

7.   **Look after Your Health:** After working, managing children and chores, and tending to the house, you feel you're exhausted and depressed. Make some time for a workout and massage. Look after your health. Going to the gym or doing physical exercise is extremely important. If you cannot do it every day, try to do it four times a week. Control your diet. Don't get emotional and overeat. Recognize your stress eating and stop it. You do not deserve an extra pastry because you're a single mother! When you look good, you'll feel good too.

8.   **Socialize:** Just because you're a single mother, it doesn't mean that you can't socialize. Go out with girlfriends for a night out once a fortnight or month. Connect with your friends on Facebook and ask them out for coffee. You need interesting adult conversations that don't revolve around work or kids. Go on a date if you want to but take things slow.

9.   **Economize:** Whether you have a spouse who gives you child maintenance or not, being a single parent means you need to curb your expenses. No more buying sexy lingerie worth thousands of rupees or splurging on diamond earrings or even shoes that you just don't need. You don't need to overspend on your child either by getting more books, toys or clothes. Keep track of your expenses. Write it in your daily calendar, journal or diary and calculate how much you spend. Don't forget a day and don't round off figures. At the end of the month, calculate. If you have a little left over, save it. You never know when you will have a rainy day and need the money. So be careful with your spending.

10. **Take Your Time:** Even if the divorce has come through, you may not be ready for a new relationship until you have let go of all the baggage from the old one. Give yourself time to heal and move on. You got into a marriage because you felt it would last forever. It did not, and you are hurt and bitter. Until you allow love to enter your life again, you should just meet friends and family members who are supportive. When you're ready to date, keep your options open. You don't need a father/mother for

your kids to replace your spouse. You need a companion for yourself. You need to feel complete in who you are and what kind of parent you are before you allow another person to enter your world. Remember that person must love and respect you and your children. Also, remember that no one is perfect. Learn from your mistakes about relationships and marriage and keep an open mind about the new one. Once you are certain about the person, introduce the children gently in a nice, kid-friendly restaurant or playground. Make sure the other person spends enough time with the kids, with you around. Talk to your children about him. The kids are not going to like the new person immediately so let them take their time to warm up to him. Remember, this new man can only be a friend to your children and not a father. Don't make him or them expect it.

Most mothers think that their children need father figures and quickly remarry and leave their children in the care of this new stranger. This is very harmful for the child as he feels you have alienated him and thinks that you're not good enough to raise him. Take your time in remarrying and first introduce your child to the man and let him feel comfortable with him in his life and his house. Your child needs you, not anyone else, to make his world complete. If your children are uncomfortable and unrelenting, reconsider remarrying. Your kids should come first.

Small sacrifices that you make today will make a huge impact tomorrow. Just be patient and calm.

I think these principles also apply to women who suddenly find themselves widowed. You need to grieve with your children and find a special corner in the house for the father. You can put up many images of the children with him, and you can spend time there recollecting stories about him. If you are terribly depressed, please seek counselling. It is a traumatic time and you don't want to pass off any negative energy to the kids who might actually be doing better than you.

Affirmation

I will stay strong for my children.

I will look after myself and give them enough time.

I will stay positive about my future ahead.